Single, Pitiful, and Unlovable…

Yeah Right!!!

Jamie M. Sorenson

Author Photo by Chelsea V Photography

ISBN: 978-0-578-41762-2 (sc)

Library of Congress Control Number: 2018913664

Dedication

To all the single, pitiful, and unlovable people out there who refuse to settle for anything but the very best for their lives, this book is for you. I hope while you're waiting to meet the love of your life, you're living a meaningful life full of purpose. When the time is right, may you be open to the love you deserve.

Acknowledgments

My deepest gratitude to God for the countless blessings, grace, and love in my life.

Special acknowledgment to the couples that role model what a great relationship should be. You teach us standards.

I would like to honor every relationship that I've had, the horrible, bad, good, and great that taught me what I needed to learn and helped me grow to become the person I am now.

Thank you to my many friends who have supported me while I was writing this book. Special thanks to Johnny C and to my late, beloved Grandma Gladys for all of her unconditional love.

A portion of the earnings from the sale of *Single, Pitiful, and Unlovable…Yeah Right!* will be donated to animal rescue and rehabilitation.

Contents

Introduction

This book is for all of the individuals who question why? Why their life is where it is? Why are they not in a relationship? What is their purpose? If you are questioning why you are single, it is likely because if you were in a relationship, it would mean that you settled, or it wasn't the right relationship for you. Perhaps you need to do a bit of work on yourself to become a better version of yourself. Possibly there's nothing wrong with you; it is simply not the right time for you to meet and be with the right person. Maybe in the bigger picture of life, there's work for you to do that you wouldn't be doing if you were committed to a relationship.

This book is for anyone who has ever asked, "What is my greatest purpose? Possibly you're in a relationship and the pearls of wisdom in my book *Single, Pitiful, and Unlovable…Yeah Right* can help improve your relationship. Maybe you need to give this book as a gift to your children and single friends who are having relationship trouble. Maybe you're a friend or family member who cares about the single people in your life enough to constantly question them and give them sometimes horrible advice about how and why to become a couple; this book is for you as well. Maybe you are questioning your purpose or you are simply looking for a fantastic book to read, then this book is for you. Prepare to be inspired.

The title of this book came about when I was asked for at least the 10,000th time why I was still single. Eventually, I started saying it's because "I'm pitiful and unlovable and obviously there's something seriously wrong with me." Immediately the person who asked me this question would say, "You're not pitiful and unlovable." Then he would start reflecting on what his question actually meant. The answer was sarcastically designed to be humorous. I simply wanted to title the book *Single, Pitiful, and Unlovable*, but I was afraid some readers wouldn't understand my sarcasm. Regardless of what my relationship status is when I finish this book, I'm happy to have lived the life I have lived.

I have worked providing mental health care for over twelve years and have learned a great deal about relationships as I have listened to thousands of people tell me their stories. Much of what I included in this book, I wish I would have known when I was younger. I chose the topics for each chapter based on relationship sagas that anyone could experience.

Although this book can be read as a standalone novel, there's a continuation from the first book in the Sarah Saga series, *Why You Tried to Kill Yourself.* For those readers who are curious about what happened with Sarah and the other characters previously, I encourage you to read *Why You Tried to Kill Yourself*. Like all of my books, it is inspiring and encouraging. My wish is that you feel validated about your life's journey, just for being the person you are meant to be after reading my books.

Don't forget authors NEED your reviews on Amazon, Barnes and Noble, Goodreads, and iBooks. So PLEASE leave reviews and tell your friends about my books so they can be inspired. Your support is much appreciated!! Part of the proceeds from Single, Pitiful and Unlovable…Yeah Right! will go to support different animal rescues.

Many Blessings,

Jamie

Sarah's Work and Travel Timeline

Age 18 -	Left Minnesota to start nursing school in Huntington Beach, CA
Age 19 -	Grandma died
Age 23-25 -	Finished nursing school and worked in Huntington Beach, CA
Age 26-27-	Started working as a traveling nurse in the U.S.A.
Age 27-28 -	Lived in Huntington Beach, CA
Age 28-31-	Lived in Italy and Turkey
Age 32-34 -	Lived in South Korea
Age 35-37-	Returned to the U.S.A.
Age 37-40-	Lived in Italy, South Korea, and Germany
Age 40-42-	Lived in Huntington Beach, CA
Age 44 -	Moved to Puerto Rico and traveled the Caribbean Islands
Age 45-	Traveled the world
Age 46 -	Returned to the U.S.A.
Age 47-	In Washington D.C. for a speech

1

∞

I Don't Understand What's Wrong with You

"Experience teaches only the teachable." – Aldous Huxley

"I don't understand what's wrong with you ladies?" Sarah's idiot boss Ralph pondered out loud for the fifth time in less than ten minutes. "Why are you still single?" Sarah and Karen felt obligated to show him a bit of Germany, but they regretted this decision almost immediately. Ralph managed the contracting company that they worked for, and he was in Germany from the U.S. checking on his employees. They were having schnitzel, spätzle with German beers, and wines at the Brauhaus am Markt tavern. The outing was fun except for the annoying questions that Ralph kept asking about why they were still single.

Karen and Sarah were excited about their upcoming trips to Brussels and Rome. Being single meant they were free to travel when they could get time off from work, and both wanted to see as much of the world as possible. Sarah was thirty-nine, and thanks to her dear friend Matthew insisting she work abroad, she had loved living and working overseas on and off since she was twenty-eight. Karen was a forty-year-old single mom. She was beautiful with long red hair, and she was a smart, passionate counselor.

Ralph couldn't help himself as he continued to ask, "What's wrong with you girls that you're still single? I thought if I spent time with you, I would be able to figure out what was wrong with you." He was oblivious to how offensive he was as he continued, "Maybe you have unrealistic standards." *What?* Thought Sarah, *this was his first time spending time with us; he doesn't know us or our standards, and he has never bothered to ask.*

Karen tried to explain, "We do date, but it's hard to meet men that we're compatible with. We have been on many dates and have tried to find a man, and for whatever reason, it hasn't worked. We've dated narcissists, players, secretly married men, men looking for a sugar mama, men with no jobs, workaholics, projects, good, and even great men, but there was no chemistry or attraction. There've been possibilities, but the timing was wrong."

Ralph didn't understand their dating plight and continued to insist, "No, there must be something wrong with you." He wasn't known for being too bright; he was tall and in great shape, and from a distance, he looked handsome. He'd done well in his career, but when he spoke, he didn't seem intelligent. Sarah secretly wondered *did he have his career success because of his image and what was assumed about him, rather than his competence? I bet his wife stays for the money.* Sarah ended Ralph's questions by saying, "We are single because we are pitiful and unlovable."

Ralph was a misogynist and ensured men were promoted over women so that they could provide good lives for their "trophy wives." He was clueless about how much he excluded women and hindered their career progression. He talked down to them and called them pet names like chickie, princess, and honey-bee. When a woman had a valid point or concern that he didn't want to hear, he would belittle her saying, "It's just a women's issue" or "Why can't y'all just be nice?" He made inappropriate comments about women's bodies, and when he was confronted, he would say, "I'm just talking about their health and fitness."

Fortunately, Sarah and Karen had contract positions with standard salaries regardless of their genders; they took overseas positions to provide patient care, to travel the world, and to experience different cultures. As Ralph continued talking, they glanced at each other with a look that said, "This is another pointless conversation; don't try to explain that there's nothing wrong with us. Perhaps, we are choosing to stay single because our lives are better this way, and the only way we will settle down is if we end up with wonderful men who enrich our lives."

When Sarah got home that night, she was pissed, and her mind was racing, *Why am I still single?*

Working through her issues

Sarah had a rough childhood but refused to have a victim mentality. Fairytales were entertaining, but that's all they were. If her dad was her mom's prince charming instead of "Then they lived happily ever after," the story would've ended, "Then Jakub ended up in prison for life for beating his wife and child to death." In order to survive, Sarah had to be strong taking care of herself and others from a young age. Growing up way too soon, she was never able to be vulnerable. Taking care of others without being cared for in return trained her brain to believe she was in this world to be used. She was a magnet for users and often didn't see it until she was badly burnt. It wasn't until she was at her most broken, dancing with death that this cycle stopped for good.

Although she appeared confident, Sarah had deep insecurities and felt unworthy when it came to a great love. Her insecurities weren't always conscious, but they manifested in her poor relationship choices. After she became secure as her own woman and understood it was okay to be vulnerable, she was ready for "the one." She wished she hadn't let fear control her and she'd been vulnerable enough to let Gabriel know how she felt about him and not waiting until a couple of days before she moved away to even talk to him. She had to learn she was lovable even if a man she wanted was unable or unwilling to love her, and he was not a bad person for not wanting her, just not the one for her.

She had to stop wasting her time being angry that she couldn't get bread from the hardwood store. Feeling like she needed to fix someone meant she didn't accept him for who he was. She had wasted so much time filling out job and college applications for men trying to make them what she wanted, not accepting them for who they were. Some of her relationships became parent-child relationships, and she exhausted herself trying to love some men enough to make them love themselves when it was a bottomless pit. She had to stop trying to understand why somebody was broken or unable to love, and the only question that mattered was, "Can he give me what I want?" After she realized her worth, she could say, "I have so much to offer; what am I getting in return?"

She had to stop disregarding guys who didn't come from the wrong side of the tracks and stop viewing them as weak because they didn't have a difficult childhood to endure. This realization included Caleb, a childhood friend who adored her, but she wouldn't give him a chance. She was glad she stopped the repeated patterns of devaluing men that she learned in childhood prior to meeting Aden.

Bad advice and making mistakes

Bad advice plus loneliness equals stupid mistakes; loneliness is powerful. Mother Teresa said, "I still think the greatest suffering is being lonely, feeling unloved, just having no one…That is the worst disease that any human being can ever experience." Sarah made many mistakes when she was lonely and didn't trust her gut. She had stupidly put her safety at risk physical, mentally, sexually, and emotionally and not protected her heart with wild intimate behavior. The consequences of these actions were a great teacher.

She had to learn to discipline herself with both her emotions and words. Words are powerful, and even logically if she might not agree or believe what she was saying, her words fed her soul and showed up in her actions. Words such as:

Opposites attract -What does that mean? If you're active and healthy, be with a couch potato? If you work hard, be with somebody who is lazy? If you're a teetotaler, be with an alcoholic? If you're generous, be with a selfish person? Opposites attract is horrible advice; you need to be with someone who you have enough similarities to be compatible with, yet different interests so you are not enmeshed so you continue to learn from each other.

You can learn to love someone. - Sarah knew people who claimed this statement to be true, and as she traveled through India, she became aware that the divorce rates with arranged marriages were lower than those of Western marriages. She had watched hundreds of murder mysteries where people killed their spouses after they experienced intense chemistry and euphoria with another person without regard to the extreme wake of destruction they caused. Obviously, this example was extreme, and the killer was a monster who elected murder over divorce. However, she was observant when individuals introduced their significant other and how their eyes lit up when they proudly said, "This is my sex puppy." Or the "I settled. This is my burden" introduction. Chemistry and attraction were essential to her and for most individuals.

Biological clock - If Sarah had a dollar for every time she heard, "Your biological clock is ticking," she could've retired and traveled the world. When she heard that statement, she wanted to say, "So you're saying I need to become impregnated by a man I don't love or desire and bring a child into the world for the selfish needs you think I should have?" If she wanted to have a child, she would've been an excellent mother, but it wasn't okay to have a baby to meet society's expectation. She wondered *will I be a mother? I want to share my life with a family; I'm just not sure how it will happen.* She had no idea the curveball life would throw her when it came to "family."

Flippant comments - "Are you thinking about what you're saying?" was what she wanted to say to the superficial thoughtless comments her closest friends said to her, such as: "You're so ambitious; you need to be with someone not as ambitious to balance you." "You work so hard; you should have someone who stays at home and cares for you." "You need to be with someone a lot different than you." "One person will be the saver and the other the spender." "One person has to be boss." "You're the woman; it's your job to take care of a man." "Give him a chance; he has potential." She felt insulted and resented these comments. Although not intentional, these statements screamed to her, "You need to settle! You're ambitious, so you need to be with someone who won't inspire you with his lack of ambition." She already took care of her home, investments, cooking, and she had a job. Why would she want someone sitting around her house all day? Why should she work hard so that a work avoidant man could waste her money? She deserved a relationship in which they took care of each other.

With all due respect to Shakespeare, she hated it when people would say, **"Expect nothing in return." Or "Don't have expectations."** How is that different than saying, "Don't have standards? Don't expect reciprocity?" What would a life look like without expectations? She had expectations for herself and for the others in her life. She held herself accountable for being a good, kind, loving, hardworking, and giving person and expected that in return. She teased Matthew relentlessly about his date with "bad hygiene girl," reminding him he was the "no expectations guy."

Sarah had been programmed to think based on her role models; even if she knew her thoughts were wrong, they were familiar and what she knew. Sarah also knew that we are programmed by the words we say. If we say, "I'm so tired," we're more tired. Even though some of her best friends were men, she treated some she dated pretty crappy in her early years justifying her actions with common statements such as: "It doesn't matter if you love him; he has money." "Men are immature." "Men can't multitask." "Men aren't emotional or sensitive." "Men don't want a strong woman." "Men just care about sex." "All men are jerks/pigs/dogs." "All men cheat." She heard common statements about women as well: "Women are emotional and overly sensitive." "Women don't care about sex." "Women are gold diggers who can't be trusted." "If you marry her, she will let herself go." "She will be your ball and chain." "As soon as you say I do, she says I don't." Then there was the "Love is the only thing that matters" comment repeatedly said by every human being until they knew better. There are few situations in which these statements could be true, but for the most part, they were generalizations that superficially justified global disrespect, while disrespecting ourselves with our words and actions. It wasn't until Sarah owned her behavior that she could change, and while it is nice to say, "Love is the only thing that matters" it's only one of the standards.

Everyone comes into your life for a reason

People come into our lives for a reason, and we can choose to learn from them even if we get hurt. When we care about someone, and the feeling isn't reciprocated, we are reminded that we are capable of caring. When we are cheated on, used, lied to, or stolen from, we know for sure that person was not the right one, and we can be more thoughtful about what to avoid in the future. There was even a purpose in Chrissy dating Charlie, the guy who blamed her for not being able to get off while he hid his porn addiction secret only able to get off with punishing friction masturbation.

Sarah thought Justin came into her life for her to show him true love, but after the heartache was over, she could see he raised her standards. She lost good guys because she felt if she gave them the praise and appreciation they deserved, she might build them up so much to the point they would think they were too good for her. She had to see how faulty this thought process was and learn to stroke a good man's ego recognizing and appreciating him.

Online dating left her asking, "If I get paid to talk to people, why would I suffer on a date for free?" "Since we have such a finite amount of time, why am I wasting it with liars, frauds, and con artists?" "If I take care of a patient with sexually deviant behavior, why would I put up with random strangers sending me dick pics through "reputable" online dating sites?"

Understanding energy and taking full responsibility for her life

Being in part raised by the wisdom Oprah shared taught her a lot of good life lessons, especially to break unhealthy cycles and take full responsibility for her life. Her childhood made her hyper-accountable in some ways, but she had to be accountable in all areas of her life. The law of attraction taught her that her actions, words, and desires must be congruent, and she would be better alone waiting to attract a winner than to be with "Mr. Alright For Now" or "Mr. Almost Right," which would repeatedly prove not to work. There couldn't be the gnawing feeling that something was missing, that she settled, or she wasn't what the man wanted.

The older she got, the more she realized how foolish she was when she bashed her past relationships. When she said, "I dated a guy, and he was such a loser." She was also saying, "Hello, my name is Sarah, and I date losers!" Or "I dated him, and he was so stupid." She was saying, "I choose to be with an idiot." She had to lecture herself saying, "You have no business dating a man you cannot have an intellectual conversation with, who does not have goals. You're hurting him with your contempt and infuriating yourself." When asked why a relationship didn't work, she learned to say, "It didn't work because we were a mismatch."

She gained insight into how unattractive she must have seemed calling men over and over after they did not respond when she chose to pick up her dog's poop rather than answer her phone as a loser was calling her again after she had already ignored his repeated calls.

She could be mentally, physically, intellectually, and sexually attracted to someone, and he could still have quirks, flaws, annoyances, and imperfections that made him human. Attraction, desire, passion, chemistry, intellectual compatibility, and respect was essential to Sarah; this included respecting his work ethic and contributions to society. So, YES! It mattered what he did for a living. She worked hard and deserved an equal.

Learning to trust her intuition as it took her where she was meant to be

Intuitively, Sarah knew she was meant to live a big life, and she would not be with the love of her life until she was older. Even when she was in the wrong relationships, she never forgot this fact. The encouragement that she received from her Grandma left her knowing that she could have or do anything. Her inner voice was loud, and she repeatedly learned to listen to it and to trust it. Sarah couldn't love halfheartedly. When she settled in a relationship, even temporarily, the gnawing feeling in her gut was unrelenting.

Sarah developed a strong faith and realized that God showed her great mercy by never letting the right person come into her life until the time was right; she had a lot of issues to work out with the wrong people as she was becoming the woman she needed to be for herself and her future soulmate. God could see how hard it was for her to be alone and gave her hope, glimpses, faith, dreams, and a feeling that love would come at the right time.

All the soul-searching Sarah did that night confirmed her boss was clueless. *Nothing is wrong with me, other than my boss is a complete idiot. I am exactly where I'm supposed to be, and there's no connecting the dots looking into the future; I have to have faith.* The author Gary Zukav was right when he said, "You cannot see in other people what you cannot experience yourself." Sarah had to see herself for exactly who she was.

2

∞

Do You Know What's Out There?

"Don't feel stupid if you don't like what everyone else pretends to love." –Emma Watson

Over seven billion people are in this world, so why was it so hard to meet somebody that you want to spend your life with? Sarah thought as she reflected on her love life. Sarah's first crush was in first grade; it lasted a day. Then the next day she had a new crush; she had a crush on every boy in her elementary school. These crushes meant sitting next to the boy at lunch and being teased about him relentlessly while denying she liked him.

In middle school, a relationship meant one person had to communicate, "Do you want to go out with me?" and the other person said, "Yes." Then they held hands in-between classes, wrote notes to each other, went to the school dances and movies together, talked on the phone, and perhaps a bit of heavy petting. Her first heartbreak was at thirteen when she saw Joseph, her boyfriend of a week, hold hands with Camille. Camille informed her, "He dumped you for me."

Drama started in high school when she and her peers became sexually active; hormones and emotions were out of control. She had boyfriends, but she quickly outgrew them; it was difficult to find someone she could stay interested in, someone with big dreams for the future. Even in high school, she intuitively knew she wanted an equal.

When she left home at eighteen with no love interest for California, it never bothered her. She wasn't meant to stay and glad nothing held her back. Caleb was the only possible potential. He was wise beyond his years with high expectations for life. He acquired his pilot's license when he was fifteen and worked odd jobs to buy his first twin-engine plane. When he was twelve, his father died from stomach cancer, and Caleb received a large trust fund as well as a gun collection that dated back before the Civil War. His mother had no interest in being a mother, and he had not seen her since he was two years old. This left him to be raised by his grandparents who were former missionaries. They raised him to be humble and wise, insisting that he study several languages and live as an international student for two years in Israel and China. His intelligence overwhelmed Sarah, and she feared she wasn't good enough for him.

Nothing ever happened between them, despite him trying several different ways to woo her. She was kind to him but rejected him nonetheless. In addition to her fear he would break her heart, her friend Eve was crazy about him. He never had any interest in Eve. After Sarah moved to Huntington Beach, California, she asked her classmates about him, but he had vanished after high school, and nobody knew what happened to him.

During her first overseas nursing assignment in Italy, Sarah was thrilled when she walked up to the nursing station to see him sitting at a desk charting notes; he was a General Surgeon. She tiptoed behind him and put her hands in his three-inch-long irresistible curly brown hair and scratched his head as she had in high school. He turned around and asked, "What are you doing?" Sarah was smiling as she said, "Caleb it is me, Sarah from high school." He shook his head and said, "I appreciate the head massage, but I'm not Caleb." Sarah didn't believe him as she continued to stare at him. He had to convince her that he wasn't Caleb and wasn't related to him. She stared at his badge and white coat where she noticed his name, "Henry Smith, M. D." The next day, she brought her high school yearbook in and showed him pictures of Caleb; he said, "He does look a lot like me, but again I'm not him. He must've meant a great deal to you." After he said that, she became obsessed with finding Caleb.

Between listening to a prior neighbor who was a detective brag constantly about all the different ways he solved cases and her experiences living abroad, she knew how to find someone. But she couldn't find Caleb or anything about him no matter how extensively she searched. She assumed he might have joined the CIA; he would've been an ideal agent. Relieved never to find his obituary, Sarah still hoped that she would find him one day.

At nineteen she lost her Grandma; the one person who she could count on completely, which abruptly changed her life, and she became serious. Dating wasn't a priority; surviving the loss of her Grandma was. She worked hard to put herself through college; she had to take full responsibility for her life if she was ever going to accomplish anything. After a year she started to date occasionally; some guys she liked, some because it was convenient, and others for the experience to date men from other cultures. At that time she didn't comprehend the pain she caused as she discarded men so easily. Sarah had to learn over and over if there is no chemistry, the relationship will NOT work no matter how great a guy is.

After college, dating coworkers was convenient rather than going out, but that led to some uncomfortable work situations. One of the most valuable life lessons she learned was jealousy is a waste of time and energy. When she was a new nurse, Taric, a wise respiratory therapist that she would run at lunch with, taught her this lesson. The first word that came to mind when looking at him and seeing how he carried himself was Machismo. However, he was incapable of being jealous. This lack of jealousy fascinated her. He told her, "If somebody is going to cheat, they'll cheat. Some of our coworkers are having sex in the storage rooms during work, and then they go home to talk to their partners about their hard work day." He pointed out different affairs going on, and she saw exactly what Taric meant. A man could legitimately need to decompress with a "guy's night out," and if he valued fidelity, that didn't change in a different environment or with the company he kept. Eliminating jealousy from her life was liberating.

That did not mean others were not jealous of her; she was a catch, and other women recognized it. Her lack of jealousy often made her oblivious to jealous women trying to sabotage her. When she was out at a club meeting men with these women and talking with a cute man, some of these women would interrupt wanting her to leave because they "didn't feel good." Some had bad mood swings acting embarrassingly rude or sexually provocative. She had to learn to set boundaries and ditch these "crazies."

Despite the "crazies," she had her best girlfriend Lynn from nursing school; they had opposite preferences in men. Every time they were together, even on their worst days, they made each other laugh hard. They motivated each other to study hard, supported and encouraged each other no matter what. They were "roll dogs," creating many crazy wild experiences as they lived life to the fullest. They stayed close regardless of what travel assignment Sarah was on and split the cost of the airline tickets when Lynn flew to see her at different stateside assignments. Huntington Beach, California was their home, but home is not always a location, rather a feeling, and Lynn was part of Sarah's foundation. Neither of them had many serious relationships. It was hard to be single and lonely, but they had each other and were as close as any sisters could be.

Male friends did a better job than her girlfriends when they set her up on a date. Men tended to be practical setting her up with men who had similar interests and attractiveness. Her girlfriends set her up with guys with potential, or they felt sorry for hoping she could help them often saving the catches for themselves. After being offended by some of the dates, she bluntly said, “I’m not a loser; I don’t need projects.”

Online dating is the way many have met the love of their life. Sarah was initially excited about how an algorithm could find an equal match with similar interests, but online dating ended up being a nightmare for her. She and a man would exchange messages, and she would be excited about meeting him only for him to stop communicating for unknown reasons. Some dates massively misrepresented themselves, anything from age, to appearance, career, education, life experiences; some had photo-shopped their pictures making them look much more attractive than they really were. On one of her dates, a man showed up who looked completely different from his online photo. The pictures on his profile were of a much more attractive man whose photos he stole from that man’s Instagram profile. She asked him, “Why did you send another person’s pictures?” He replied, “You might think I was ugly.” She was bewildered, and after a few moments said, “Well, now I think you’re unattractive and a liar.”

After that, video communication was a must before meeting a man she had met online; most men avoided video communication, yet they were quick to send her a picture of a dick, presumably theirs. They had a classy profile, then after a couple of greetings or in some cases before the communication started, they would send her a picture of an erect penis with a caption that read something like, "Interested?" This disrespectful behavior was sickening; in some cases, she was paying for online dating services only to be extremely disrespected. She thought *if I wanted to be disrespected sexually, I could be paid for it rather than paying to meet these perverts, married men acting single, liars and so on.*

Her final online dating experience was when she was thirty-seven and working in Italy the second time. Rick was an American Federal Law Enforcement Agent. He was cute enough, definitely interesting and savvy about international living. She wasn't sure if she was attracted to him and took it slow. He took her slow pace as a challenge, a brick wall to climb and went out of his way to impress her with amazing dates visiting beautiful cathedrals, historical sites, major attractions, driving through the countryside to quaint villages, and dining in romantic restaurants.

In his quest to impress her, he talked nonstop which exhausted her after listening to patients all day. Sarah would've enjoyed quiet time together. It was especially disgusting when he talked with his mouth full of food. She appreciated his efforts, but she never developed a great deal of interest in him. His stories also didn't add up, especially relating to his age and the timeline when these supposed events occurred. His profile said he was forty-three, and he looked forty-three. On their last date as he was rambling on, he mentioned he was forty, and she quickly said, "I thought you were forty-three." He responded her, "No, you're confused; I'm forty."

As the day passed, she asked about his family, and he talked about his eighty-six-year-old mother and his sister who was nine years younger than him. Sarah asked, "So your Mom was fifty-five when she had your sister?" Rick started stumbling over his words claiming they had the same dad but not the same mom even though that contradicted his earlier story. They were having a nice dinner and were going to take a gondola afterward, so in the interest of enjoying the moment, Sarah made a mental note of his inconsistencies and changed the subject. While on the gondola, he put his arms around her, and her entire body cringed as every cell felt repulsed; her ovaries jumped into her lungs. He didn't realize she was looking down at his backpack only to see his wallet as he talked nonstop. She discretely flipped it open and looked at his driver's license to see he was fifty-three. She then told him, "I don't feel well, and I need to go home after we get off of the gondola." He took her home and tried to get her to invite him in; she politely and firmly said, "No" and avoided a make-out session by telling him, "I don't want to get you sick, but thank you for the nice date."

Once inside, she looked at the screenshots she had taken of his profile before their first date which showed he was forty-three. The next day she drove to his work to confront him about his lies. At least he hadn't lied about his job; he had taken her to his office on their first date because he supposedly forgot something. He knew many women are attracted to men who work in law enforcement, and taking her to his work was his not so covert way to impress her. As she was driving up to his office, she saw him outside smoking which infuriated her. Smoking was a deal breaker, no exceptions. He was the one who initially talked about how much he disliked cigarette smoke and would have them reseated if someone was smoking near them. He was a complete fraud; any additional conversation was a waste of time and energy, so she continued driving; luckily, he hadn't seen her.

She went home packed up everything he had given her, waited until he was off work, and then dropped off the box with the desk sergeant. She handed the box to the attractive sergeant asking him, “Will you please give with this box to Rick?” She wished she had dated him instead; maybe he wouldn’t have been a pathological liar.

She ignored Rick’s calls and text messages as she did a ZABA online people search of him. This website listed his birthday the same as his driver’s license; she was sure he was fifty-three. She texted him a screenshot of his profile that said he was forty-three and a screenshot of ZABA showing his age to be fifty-three; then she texted, “Happy early fifty-fourth birthday. Don’t ever contact me again!!!!”

He harassed her calling and texting her nonstop, using gaslighting techniques saying, “You’re crazy, I’m thirty-nine. How could you come up with this delusion that I’m fifty-three?” She didn’t respond as his communication became more aggressive, showing how unstable he was. Sarah was worried that he might try to harm her, and she took an unplanned vacation to Istanbul, Turkey to get away from him.

After she arrived in Istanbul, she sent all of his messages to his superiors as well as an impassioned letter discussing her safety concerns. She wasn’t sure what happened to him, but the gaslighting stopped, and she never heard from him again. She wondered *how could he have expected to have a relationship built completely on lies? How could she ever have authentic intimacy with somebody she can’t trust?* After the dick pictures, deception, and Rick, she was discouraged about what was out there.

In Istanbul, she treated herself to a gorgeous hotel near the Bosporus and slept for fourteen hours after checking in; Rick and his lies had exhausted her. The next day, she toured the markets and attractions. There was so much to experience in food, entertainment, mansions, beautiful architecture, and so on. As she sat at an outdoor restaurant eating a combination platter of olives, figs, grilled tomatoes, cucumbers, hummus, and lava puff bread with a side of baklava, she looked up and saw Caleb. She knew for sure it was him; he was staring at her. She couldn't believe it and waved at him as a group of people walked in front of him. As soon as the group passed, he was gone. Maybe her mind was playing tricks on her as a relief from the recently endured misery? But it definitely seemed real. The waiter asked, "Are you okay? You look like you saw a ghost." She handed the waiter enough liras to cover the bill and a hefty tip. Abandoning her food, Sarah ran over to where she saw Caleb frantically trying to find him, but he had disappeared. After searching for a couple of hours, she resumed her sightseeing, but she could only think of him.

That night sitting in the café at her hotel overlooking the Bosporus drinking cay, a lovely Turkish tea, Sarah was trying to sort her thoughts when the waiter approached her with a glass of Masseto Toscana wine. She said, "I didn't order this." He replied, "The American man at the bar bought it for you." She looked over at the empty bar. The waiter looked back at the bar and was as puzzled as she was. He said, "I thought he knew you; he paid for your tea as well."

She knew the man at the bar had to be Caleb. After twenty years, he looked the same, only a bit more mature. She wondered if her suspicion that he was in the CIA was right, and it was his way of letting her know he recognized her while also being discreet. She finished her tea and wine then walked into the hotel lobby where she was stopped by a bellman who handed her beautiful flowers with a card. She opened the card thinking *this is absolutely crazy. If it was Caleb, I rejected him in high school. Why would he send me flowers and buy me expensive wine?* She opened the card and read, "Hello to the one that got away." Now she thought *he's messing with my head.*

She couldn't sleep, and around five A.M., there was a light tap at her door. She opened it to see Caleb standing there looking impeccable. Her first thought was *I look like a mess with bead hair in my pajamas.* She asked, "What's going on? How did you know I was here? Why didn't you talk to me yesterday? Why do you keep disappearing? It is wonderful to see you by the way." He replied, "I would've loved to talk to you, but I was in the middle of taking care of some business. Can we talk now over breakfast?" "Sure, let me get ready," she replied. He looked so nice; she was embarrassed she didn't have better clothes with her. "Great! Get ready. I'll be back in fifteen minutes; I know you're not a diva," he teased. They both laughed. It was true; she was extremely efficient even in high school. She was known to take a shower and do her hair and makeup in under ten minutes.

He took her to an intimate café where they were the only customers. Over a five-hour breakfast, they talked nonstop. He seemed to know a bit about her life over the past twenty years without her saying anything. Later that day, she called Lynn to tell her what happened. Lynn asked her a lot of basic questions about him, but Sarah didn't have the answers. Reflecting back on their conversation, she didn't know much about his current life or what he had done the past several years.

Sarah told Lynn, "I assume he had his reasons for being guarded; after all, I was the one who rejected him. Maybe if I opened up to him, he will do the same." As they were about to end their conversation, the doorbell rang. Sarah opened the door and the bellman handed her a package. Lynn insisted, "Open it now." In the box were three gorgeous dresses, two pairs of high heels, and matching jewelry. Lynn asked, "Is it from the guy you rejected?" Sarah said, "Well, who else?" A note in the box read, "I'll meet you in the lobby at 1700; I'm taking you to a fancy restaurant. You're beautiful no matter what, but you might be more comfortable in one of these dresses."

The dresses looked amazing on her; they were classy and sexy but not overly provocative. When she exited the elevator, Caleb was waiting in the lobby. Her heart skipped a beat when she saw him; he was so handsome. The restaurant was expensive, but it didn't seem like he was trying to impress her. This restaurant seemed to be standard for him. As they finished dinner, they stared at each other in silence. Her heart was pounding, and she felt butterflies for the first time in a long time; he also seemed nervous despite his confidence. She broke the silence and said, "I'm going to say what I should've years ago. I liked you a lot when you asked me out in high school, but I was afraid that you were out of my league and would break my heart. I'm sorry I never went out with you; I deeply regret that now. I always admired you and thought you were incredible."

He was taken aback by her honesty as his eyes teared up. He was finally validated by her. He reached out for her hands; nothing was said, but the connection was strong, and he felt like home. That night they finally kissed, twenty years later. It was magical.

They spent the next two days together as he showed her Istanbul; the beauty of some of the Mosques was breathtaking. He told her all about the city, and they were so busy taking in all of the sights and living in the moment that she ignored all of the questions Lynn kept texting her to find out. "Where does he live?" "What does he do for work?" He mentioned he owned security companies and traveled so much he was never at home. Sarah didn't feel like interrogating him as they sat cuddled up in the silence. The familiarity and connection were all she thought she needed.

After spending their third day together and only a few hours apart each night, he asked, "Do you want to spend the night with me?" She couldn't say yes fast enough; she wasn't promiscuous, but she wanted to spend every minute with him. She hadn't been this happy in years. He took her to a mansion right on the Bosporus and told her it was a short-term rental while he was in Istanbul on business; the mansion was magnificent. They snuggled up and drank wine; the night was better than any fantasy. She felt completely at peace, safe and secure as she fell asleep in his arms with her head on his chest. Right before she dozed off, she noticed he held her extra tight and had a look of deep sadness in his eyes that she didn't understand.

She slept more soundly than she had in years. She woke up refreshed and reached for him. He was gone with only a note on his side of the bed that read, "Sarah, I've always loved you. C" She turned the note over, and it read, "Someday." She jumped out of bed and searched the mansion for him; there wasn't a trace he had ever been there. She went back and looked at the note and under the note was a white gold necklace with a pendant of the Archangel Gabriel, the messenger angel. She wondered *what message is this supposed to be?* She was confused and utterly devastated. A house attendant arrived, and she felt out of place being there, so she dressed quickly getting ready to leave. The attendant knocked on the door and asked, "Can I get you anything, Ms. Sarah?" She opened the door asking, "How do you know my name?" The attendant looked confused and said, "My boss told me to make sure you had everything you wanted. We also have a car and a driver here to take you anywhere until you have to fly out on Friday." Sarah asked, “Is Caleb your boss?” The attendant said, “No Ma’am, I don’t know Caleb.” Sarah spent her last two days in Istanbul trying to wrap her head around what had happened. *Who was Caleb? Why did he disappear? Where is he? He seemed to care about me, but then he left without a goodbye or an explanation* were some of the thoughts that played over and over in Sarah’s mind. She was disenchanted; the “what happened” and “why” questions haunted her.

She returned to Italy; she was done justifying why she was still single. It was exhausting. The people who cared the most about her were often the most critical. All she would say was, “Do you know what’s out there?”

3

∞

Settling…Would You Want to be with You?

"It's better to be healthy alone than sick with someone else." –Phil McGraw

We are all connected and need to hold on to the treasured individuals in our lives. It was nine years after Sarah cared for Raul during the worst time in his life, when he had thought suicide was the best option until they crossed paths again. He was happier now than he could have ever imagined and contributed a lot of his happiness to her making him be honest when he was her patient on a mental health unit all those years before. His truth led to living an authentic life. There was no way he was going to let running into her be a random encounter and insisted they stay in touch. Their friendship grew, and she got to know his husband, Pavlo; his parents, Maria and Hector; his daughter, Mercedes, as well as his ex-wife, Erica. They all embraced her and made her a part of their family, which she appreciated, as she had been estranged from her own family for years.

She never talked much about her family, but Maria recognized there must've been a lot of pain for someone with her depth of character to walk away. Maria and Hector went out of their way to make her feel welcome; they were grateful for her impact on Raul's life.

Sarah and Erica became friends as they volunteered to move a lady in need from one apartment to another. Erica was outgoing, and they chatted while moving boxes. After that day, Sarah frequently got supportive and encouraging text messages from Erica. She was delighted to receive this thoughtful gesture as she was normally the supporter and encourager.

Matthew was another gem who she held on to; he was her chosen little brother, fellow nurse, and traveler. She met her best friend Johnny who became her most trusted confidant when he was her patient shortly after becoming a nurse. She had no idea who he was other than a patient with a ruptured appendix who refused medical treatment until he was near death. She learned over time he has a wealthy businessman who owned hotels and restaurants throughout the South West corner of the United States. He was a workaholic and getting medical care took away from his work, so when his appendix ruptured he tried to deny the pain until he passed out, and his secretary called 911. He was admitted after surgery to the medical surgical ward she worked for I.V. antibiotics to ensure he didn't develop sepsis and for pain control treatment. Sarah was working the night shift, and the day shift nurse reported, "He is almost completely silent as a patient, just working from his laptop and not asking for anything." Sarah questioned, "Well how much pain medicine are you giving him?" The day shift nurse replied, "None, he is not asking for any." This neglect pissed Sarah off; surely, he must be in pain, and the nurse's job was to advocate for the patient. Sarah let the day shift nurse know that she was aggravated at her for not being more invested in caring for her patient.

After the change of shift nursing report, Sarah walked into Johnny's room and inquired, "What's this monkey business I hear about you not taking any pain medication?

Especially after you were near death before you received medical care? Not on my watch, I don't want my patients to suffer needlessly." Like Raul, Johnny immediately respected her and agreed to let her give him pain medication. He felt safe with her and was hugely relieved to be out of pain. She took excellent care of him, recognizing he was incredibly guarded and reserved but a good soul. They visited when she could during the night shifts and played a hand or two of cards on the slow nights.

After he was discharged from the hospital, they met about once a week for happy hour, dinner, or sometimes breakfast. He was eighteen years older than her, and he was like a protective older brother. She was one of the only people he made personal time for; even if it was a phone call, he was there for her and visited her a couple of times on her travel assignments. He told her, "What I love the most about you is that I can count on you to do what you say and to be honest. You cared for me when I was at my most vulnerable. Do you know how hard it is to find someone you can trust like that?" He never got close to people because most wanted to use him. Despite being a powerful businessman and a multimillionaire, he was humble. He made huge anonymous donations to animal rescue groups and programs for foster children. Their mutual passion for animal rescue further bonded their friendship.

When Sarah was in Huntington Beach, California, she and Lynn were frequently together. Lynn hated that Sarah always felt the need to move but supported her endeavors. Lynn wouldn't travel overseas but frequently called to ask, "When are you coming home, young lady?" Erica loved to travel, and she and Raul were great co-parents. Knowing Mercedes was being well cared for during her time with her dads, freed Erica to take foreign journalism assignments.

In addition to the States, Sarah had lived and worked in Italy, South Korea, Germany, and Turkey. She returned to Italy when she was thirty-seven for a second travel assignment there. Serendipitously, Erica took an assignment in Germany to report on the refugee migration at the same time Sarah was in Italy. Sarah was thrilled they were only a two-hour flight apart. Erica was a ball of energy, quick to get excited and emotional, one of the most thoughtful people Sarah had ever met. She had mostly gotten over the pain of her divorce from Raul, but she still had trust issues. The love of her life and father of her child was gay, and she had been betrayed.

Erica met Adal, a local German man eight years younger than her, a few days after she arrived in Germany. He asked her to go on a date, and she agreed. She preferred younger energetic men, and he could show her Germany from his perspective. Dating wouldn't be serious as she was only there a short time and then would return home to Mercedes.

She could not have foreseen how toxic of an environment she would be working in. Wesley, her supervisor, was a monster with serious mommy issues which morphed into a hatred for women. Being overseas in an isolated area made it easier for him to get away with abuse and for headquarters to overlook what he was doing. He created a hostile and abusive environment leaving her exhausted and beaten down. Headquarters ignored her reports of abuse, so she documented the abuse in order to file a substantial complaint against him when she returned to protect future individuals who worked for him. She also planned on doing a major story on workplace bullies and the damage they can do with their power and control based on her firsthand experience.

She hoped Adal would be a fun distraction to take her mind off the abuse and loneliness that was taking its toll on her. Adal was educated and had a good job. They had exchanged witty banter since they had met but hadn't gone on a date. Finally, Erica asked, "What happened to you taking me on that date?" He picked her up a couple of nights later and took her to dinner. Throughout dinner, he seemed shy as they talked about their different travels around the world; she was much more traveled and experienced, but he had the insight on the local culture.

As he dropped her off at her home, she hugged him and thanked him for dinner. He leaned in and kissed her. It was one of those bad kisses where he missed her mouth and kissed her nose and then re-aimed smashing his teeth into hers. The kiss was disappointing, but she thought *I'm lonely, and he's nice enough and decent looking.*

Over the week, they continued to exchange witty messages, and he asked her, "Do you want to go on another date?" She agreed, and he suggested the same boring restaurant with the mediocre food they went on for their first date. She thought the only reason they went there before was because it was convenient. She agreed telling herself, "A date is about getting to know someone, not where you get to know them." He was well read so he could hold his own in a conversation. There wasn't a spark or fireworks for her, but she had missed intimacy for a long time and was giving it a shot. They had a make-out session after the second date, which was slightly better than the first kiss. She wondered *can the fun energy of the text messages transcend into other areas of his life?* The first date was on a Tuesday, and their second was on a Saturday. At the end of the date, he asked, "Do you want to come back here on Tuesday?" She was disappointed, but her German colleagues assured her some German men are creatures of habit.

Erica texted him later saying, "I'm okay with a third date but not at the same restaurant. Let's try something new." Adal texted back, "I need time to process this idea. I'll think about it and text you back." This text was odd; she was fun and spontaneous and never met anyone who needed time to decide if he would try a new restaurant. The next day he called to say, "We can try a new restaurant on Tuesday."

Wesley had messed up a major project, and Erica had to stay at work so late that she couldn't make it for her third date to the restaurant before it closed. Adal had driven to see her, so she suggested that they watch a movie at her flat. He brought a nice bottle of wine, and they cuddled and laughed at the comedy that was playing. She had been celibate for a while, and one thing led to another, and they ended up having sex. It was the most sexually disappointing experience that she ever had. He lasted two and a half thrusts, about two seconds. He was oblivious of how bad he was as he bragged, "I'm huge." She was thinking, *your weapon might be average, but you're no warrior with it.*

The next day she complained to Oscar, her gay American coworker who had lived in Germany for the past year. He was also from Mexico and understood the cultural differences she was dealing with. He told her, "Honey, don't forget that you're a passionate Latina woman, dating a much younger rule-oriented German boy. You need to show him the ropes." She sighed, "You're probably right, but it's not what I want to hear. I'm in his home country; I want him to show me castles and take me to Oktoberfest, the Christmas markets, Wine Route, or Deutsche Weinstrasse. I don't want to be a teacher." Adal seemed decent, so she ignored her lingering disappointment.

Later that day, he texted her saying, "I want to confirm we are getting together on Saturday? Do you want to watch movies at your flat?" She responded, "Absolutely not, I want to go out and explore Germany. If you want to go out, you need to come up with something fun." Adal replied, "I need a couple of days to process this idea." *What?* She thought. *How could being spontaneous be that difficult?* She used the cultural differences as an excuse to justify her disappointment, and even though the sex was bad, she craved intimacy, cuddling, and sleeping next to someone.

Friday morning, he texted her saying, "I found a festival for us to go to tonight." This message was great news for her since she was having a miserable day. Wesley took every chance he could to yell at her; even though he wasn't rational in his rants the verbal abuse was horrible. Earlier that day, he demanded to speak to her in the middle of interviewing a man who was a refugee from Afghanistan. She apologized to the man and went to see what was so important. Wesley said, "I wanted to tell you, I have the power to ruin you as a reporter." She knew this statement wasn't true, and she was aware he was hated and seen as a joke in the broadcasting community. Erica asked, "Where's this threat coming from? I work hard and make you look good. I'm a respected and accomplished reporter." He replied, "I just wanted to remind you that I have power over you." He had previously managed to jeopardize her pay and she went weeks before she got paid.

She finished the interview and went back to her office. Wesley strolled in her office uninvited acting nice and charming as he asked her, "Why don't you ask more about me? You're a journalist; it's your job to ask people their stories." His presence made her nauseous; the thought of knowing him better repulsed her. At social functions, he lied about having credentials, accomplishments and experiences he did not have, while trying to read her face wondering if she would expose him. She pitied his wife who he kept constantly pregnant and dependent on him.

Going to a festival was just what Erica needed. Festivals included good food, drinks, Glühwein - German mulled wine, dancing, music, shopping, and costumes. She praised Adal several times for coming up with such fun plans for them. After the festival, they went back to her flat, and he initiated sex. She wore sexy lingerie hoping to spice things up and hopefully sex would be a little better. He lasted nine seconds and finished like he completed a masterpiece. She thought *you have to be freaking kidding me.* Eventually, she seductively said, "It's nice to date a guy that's eight years younger than me. I think that might mean you have more stamina." She winked at him and started to caress him, hoping round two might last long enough for her to get some satisfaction. He pushed her away saying, "You're putting too much pressure on me. I can handle sex two times a week, once on Tuesday and once on Saturday, and this Friday was an exception."

She was dumbfounded. He pulled her back on his chest, and she straddled him as he took care of business with his fingers. In spite of the premature ejaculation, he had satisfying finger skills. She wasn't sure what to do; clearly the relationship wasn't satisfying, but neither was being lonely. She didn't know if she would see him on again or not. She wouldn't give him an answer about if she was free to meet him or not, if it was even worth her time.

Tuesday came, and Wesley was in full force strutting around like he was some type of god to be worshiped, oblivious of how people instantly disliked him calling him the village idiot behind his back. He had upset their German coworkers creating a hostile working relationship between the Americans and the Germans. He demanded Erica fix everything. Even the biggest misogynist found how Wesley treated her deplorable. She did everything she could to stay away from him, any work trip, offsite project; she used all of her vacation time. Every day she didn't have to interact with him, she did a five-minute dance. She repeatedly called headquarters letting them know about his abuse and extreme incompetence and let them know she would be filing a complaint when this assignment was over. Headquarters didn't take her seriously and later regretted that decision when Sarah would do an anti-bullying campaign and referred to this situation and the apathetic leadership who could have stopped the abuse. They greatly underestimated the value of a pissed off friend, but that's another story. Erica endured the abuse for two reasons: there was great purpose in the stories she reported; she understood the unique difficulties immigrants faced, and she planned on reporting on workplace bullying in the future.

As a distraction, she met Adal at the usual restaurant, and Erica asked, "Isn't it boring to go to the same restaurant all of the time, and why don't we ever go to your flat?" He replied, "I still live with my parents." This response shouldn't have surprised her, but it did; he was twenty-nine. He saw her facial expression and said, "It is normal in Germany to live with your parents until you get married." She wasn't sure if she believed him. He then asked, "How was your day?" She started to cry, and he comforted her by holding her hand and rubbing her back, exactly what she needed.

She remained torn about what to do; the relationship was unsatisfying, but occasionally she got what she needed. Was this relationship enough, even for a short-term relationship with an expiration date? She taught him a lot about sex, and with time, it was a little better. She longed for the passion that she had with previous lovers, but he was safe. She questioned his rules at times, but he would say, "I'm German, and that's the way it is." That wasn't what she saw from other Germans. He had six weeks of mandatory vacation annually; she had much less but made every second count. She asked him, "Do you want to go to Paris for a couple days?" He replied, "I'm too tired." She thought *he is not tired, just lazy.*

She went to Paris alone and saw happy couples as she explored the attractions. While having dinner at Calife, a magnificent restaurant with 360-degree views of Paris, she met a German man who she talked to for about an hour, and then he invited her to tour the German wine Strasse with him sometime. Erica could tell he was romantically interested in her and was fun and spontaneous, like her. She told him, "I'm sorry, I'm in a relationship." She and Adal agreed to be exclusive after they started having sex. She then called Adal excited about the possibility of driving through the wine Strasse and going to Oktoberfest with him. He said unenthusiastically, "I would rather stay home and watch a movie." She asked, "What should I expect if I go alone again?" He responded, "I don't know. I've never been." His lack of adventure and enthusiasm was turning her off.

When she returned from Paris, her coworker had sprained his ankle and was unable to go on a prepaid snowboarding trip to Switzerland, so he gave Erica his tickets. She was excited to go to Switzerland for free and called Adal asking, "Do you want to go on an all-expense paid snowboarding trip to Switzerland? It's an amazing opportunity!" He responded in an annoyed tone, "You know I'm flat-footed, and I don't snowboard."

She was fed up. While snowboarding in Switzerland, she met Luca, a handsome Italian snowboard instructor; they raced down the hills challenging each other to new levels with challenging runs and jumps. Luca invited her to dinner. She agreed saying, "Yes, but I'm dating someone, so no romance." Luca replied, "I'm disappointed you have a boyfriend, but I still would like your company." Over dinner, he asked, "Why is your boyfriend not here? Do you and he have fun together? You seem like a passionate woman." She sat across from Luca thinking, *Adal isn't fun or exciting, and he's a lousy lover. So why am I dating him? Why am I settling even for a short period of time? He is safe, reliable and he provides a bit of comfort on bad days.*

She smiled at Luca and said, "I need to go before I do something I regret." She wouldn't compromise her values no matter how attractive Luca was. She knew what she had to do. After she broke up with Adal and was done working in Germany, she flew to Italy to spend time with Sarah. Much of their time together, Sarah built Erica back up after Wesley had demoralized her. Sarah cooked for her, hugged her while she cried, and made sure the home was quiet and peaceful, so Erica could get restorative sleep.

Heart to heart conversation

Both of them believed everything happened for a reason, and good could come out of adversity. They had a lot of deep conversations and talked a great deal about why life works out the way it does. As they were talking, Sarah said, "I have a brilliant idea, we could use both of our skill sets and do some serious anti-bullying work. Use what was meant to break and ruin us to help others as well as expose bullies for who they are."

They were such great friends they asked each other for honest feedback about making improvements in their life to become better people. They wanted to be their best and attract the best. They both provided kind, gentle input with good intentions knowing steel sharpens steel. Sarah talked about the dangers of settling even for short periods as it subconsciously trains the mind to settle.

Sarah asked, "Do you see ways I can improve my life?" Erica said, "I'm glad you asked because you're dressing like an old lady, and you need to put more work into your appearance. You can spend more time on your hair and makeup and wear nicer clothes. I don't know if perhaps you're depressed, but you're not taking care of yourself like I remember. You used to make yourself up and wear sexy clothes; you were twisted steel and sex appeal. I am telling this to you with love; you're beautiful but look tired."

Sarah was a bit hurt by this honesty, but the truth was she was always tired, and she wasn't sure why. She loved her pajamas and a soft bed more than anything after work. Perhaps the years of traveling and working long hours had taken its toll? Or she had caregiver fatigue and was burnt out? She considered taking a year off and going down to the Caribbean Islands to rest and relax and get her strength back. She had saved enough to take a year off. She appeared to have as much energy as the average person, but average wasn't her baseline. She mentioned her exhaustion and unexplained pains in her body to her doctor. He ran a plethora of tests and couldn't find anything wrong. He concluded, "Maybe you're just getting older." Sarah said, "Maybe you're right, and I'm a hypochondriac." In her heart, she knew he wasn't right.

They encouraged each other to keep the faith, not to settle, and keep their most important character virtues of generosity, courage, flexibility, adventure, honesty, humor, intelligence, kindness, loyalty, optimism, benevolence, and tolerance, which they both had. Erica asked, "Do you think we're too strong and too independent?" Sarah rolled her eyes asking, "How many times have we heard that from a man with low expectations? Maybe our strength and independence are intimidating because they know they would have to step into a league that maybe they could not handle, so something must be wrong with us. We have no time to waste with apathetic MFs trying to drag us down."

Erica told Sarah, "You have a warm, loving, giving heart, and people feel safe with you, but you tend to attract users. These people are not aware of how self-centered they are. Most people are not intuitive enough to realize once they push you too far or take advantage of you, one to many times you're done with them. I don't even think you're aware of your empathic energy, and you think people should know not to take advantage, but they don't. Sarah, you're a dis-engager and just like people get hurt when they're cheated on, people get hurt when you walk away. You don't even talk about it with them. You reach your threshold, and you're done. I've seen you withdraw from people who consider you to be their best friend." Sarah only partially agreed with her and defended herself saying, "I do talk about it and what's unacceptable. I am honest about my history of leaving relationships when the imbalance of give and take got to be too much." "Yes, Sarah, you talk, you talk in a soft, gentle manner even when you're mad, and people don't realize you're mad because you're so controlled. You realize the importance of words more than other people; look at the work you do. You have to control your emotions and remain calm, but most people don't. They hear you saying this is not okay, but you do not appear to be mad or emotional, so they don't take you seriously. You expect people to have insight into their own behavior and most don't. They don't realize they're pushing you away or why you walked away. I don't think that's fair." Maybe Erica was hitting a nerve or Sarah didn't agree, but she ended the conversation saying, "I'm not a teacher. If I have to teach a friend or a lover not to be selfish and realize a relationship is not just about them, I don't need them. My long-term relationships are balanced and healthy, especially with Johnny. We have supported each other through everything. Relationships are supposed to be easy."

Sarah didn't understand why she was a user magnet. Sarah then said, "Let's talk about you being so afraid of being hurt that you close your heart to a real romance in the name of self-preservation. You make men jump through hoops to prove that they're good enough and set them up for failure with unrealistic expectations. One of those men that you're putting through the ringer could be an amazing man, but he sees you as high maintenance. When you like a guy, you have to let your guard down and say, "I miss you; I'm thinking about you." Men and women are different when it comes to ego. Giving a man a compliment is like putting Miracle Grow on a plant. It does not matter if we hold our love inside or show it, it still exists. If we're going to lose someone who wasn't meant to be ours, we still get hurt even if we hide how much we care. The difference is we regret not saying what we needed to say."

Both women hit on nerves with the best of intentions; it was a relief when Raul called to check on them and let Mercedes talk to Erica. Erica missed her and couldn't wait to see her. It was very hard to be away. Erica thought about how hard it must be on parents in the military who deploy for up to a year at a time away from their children.

4

∞

I Want You to Meet My Friend

"I've learned over the years to appreciate God's timing, and you can't rush things; it's gonna happen exactly when it's supposed to." –Sevyn Streeter

As Erica was saying goodbye to Mercedes, Matthew was FaceTiming in. Erica answered and was surprised to see such a handsome man. He was also taken aback by her. He asked, "Did I call the wrong number?" She said, "Oh no, I'll get Sarah." He asked Sarah, "Did you want to explore Rome today?" Sarah replied, "That sounds great; let me ask Erica." Sarah looked at Erica and asked, "I want you to meet my friend; he's inviting us to explore Rome. Do you want to go?" Erica made sure she wasn't on FaceTime and nodded enthusiastically.

Matthew had been an Army nurse who deployed to Afghanistan for a year then was stationed in Germany where he learned about contract nursing. After getting out of the Army, he worked with Sarah on a stateside travel assignment and introduced her to overseas contract nursing assignments. He was fun, humble, and had more than his fair share of pain in life. There was never any romantic chemistry between them. When Sarah introduced him to Erica, she felt like she was introducing her little brother.

Matthew came over to Sarah's flat and sat on the couch as he began to tell Sarah, "I have several ideas for what we are going to do today." Sarah loved that he was a planner and took responsibility to contribute to their adventures. He had no idea what fate had in store for him that day. He told Sarah, "We are going to spend a couple of hours in the Vatican City, a couple of hours in the Musei Vaticani, then on to the Sistine Chapel, but we can only be there three hours. There's an outdoor restaurant across from the Colosseum for dinner, and then we can walk around the Colosseum." Sarah groaned, "That will be a twelve-hour day; I can't handle all of that and work a twelve to fourteen-hour shift tomorrow." Matthew confidently declared, "We got this."

When Erica "the diva" finished getting ready and walked into the living room, Matthew stopped talking and stared at her; she was even more beautiful in person. Erica stared back as she sat on Sarah's glass table top causing the glass to flip up and the cups on the table to fall and break. Sarah asked, "Are you hurt?" Erica immediately said, "No, I'm sorry for breaking the cups." Sarah was easy-going and didn't care. Matthew immediately started helping Erica clean up the glass as he said, "Hi, I'm Matthew." Erica giggled, "I figured; I'm Erica."

They left the flat and got into Matthew's car. Erica chattered incessantly to ease her nerves, and Matthew was mostly frozen with nervous silence as they kept exchanging glances. They were like "twitterpated" teenagers. Sarah wasn't sure if their giddiness was cute or annoying, but she did know this type of chemistry was incredibly rare, so she tried to be both invisible as well as a conversation guider when needed.

As they explored, Matthew tried to impress Erica with different historical facts. Sarah felt like a third wheel and kept making excuses to step away giving them a chance to get to know each other. They didn't get home until almost midnight making it a fifteen-hour day; Sarah was exhausted but did her best to contain her grouchiness. Sarah played it pretty cool all day long, but realizing how nervous they were so she said, "You two should stay in touch. I'm going to bed."

Erica and Matthew talked outside for another thirty minutes. When Matthew finally left, Erica burst into Sarah's room flopped onto the bed as she put her head into a pillow and screamed as she kicked her feet up and down on the bed, obviously waking up Sarah who sat up asking, "Have you lost your mind?" Erica hugged her and said, "Not my mind, but maybe my heart. How could you not have told me about him? I'm so excited; I've never had butterflies like this. Please tell me he is straight?" Sarah laughed and said, "100 percent and I've told you about him at least one hundred times." Erica kept talking about how she hadn't felt like this before.

She then interrogated Sarah with multiple questions about him: "Has he ever been married? Does he have a girlfriend? How could someone like that be single? Does he have any kids? Has he ever been in love? Is he a player? Would he be okay dating a woman who lives in the States and has a daughter? Would he consider moving to Houston? Is he intimidated by successful women? Does he have financial or drug problems? Is there any chance he's a porn addict? What do you know about him? Has anything ever happened between the two of you?" The questions kept coming, and Sarah reminded her about the earlier self-preservation conversation and said, "Don't sabotage this. Matthew is a great guy who has had a hard time finding the right girl. He has his own trust issues, but he should tell you about those." Erica wanted to stay up and talk all night; her heart was pounding. Sarah had to get up in four hours, so she sent Erica out of the room. Erica continued to fantasize about the possibilities about her life with Matthew. Sarah was thinking *life is crazy; it can change in a moment. Eighteen hours earlier Erica was crying and complaining that there was nothing on the horizon; now she was on cloud nine.*

Erica was making breakfast, dressed to the nines looking gorgeous in her sexy outfit, expensive perfume, and her makeup perfectly done when Sarah walked out at five A.M. Sarah laughed as she said, “If you're going to come here and make me breakfast, come and visit more often.” Erica winked at her and said, “That's fine I could get to know Matthew better.”

When Sarah got out of the shower, Matthew was sitting in the living room. He stood up and said, “I thought we could commute to work today because you haven’t had that inspection done on your car, and I brought breakfast.” Sarah started to say, “We already,” but Erica interrupted her saying, “That was so thoughtful of you, let’s eat.” Sarah rolled her eyes without them seeing.

After her second breakfast, she and Matthew were late to work. Late was normal for her but never Matthew. Erica hugged Sarah and said, “Have a great day.” Erica then hugged Matthew; they both had huge smiles. As they walked to the car, Sarah said, “Easter is coming up; we should all fly to Santorini, Greece if Erica is willing to do another international trip.” Erica immediately shouted, “That sounds great; let's do it.” Erica was embarrassed by her reaction realizing how loud she was; Matthew smiled and said, “I'm game.”

On the way to work, Sarah asked Matthew, “What inspection do I need to get?” Matthew said, “Don’t say anything; your next tune-up is on me. Thanks for playing it cool.” He went on to say, “How could you not have told me about her? She's amazing. I like her. She's probably out of my league; I looked her up online last night; she's kind of a famous reporter. Do you think there's any chance a guy like me would have a chance with her? How do you know her? Why haven't I met her before? How long has she been single? I bet she has hundreds of men after her."

Sarah smiled and shook her head and said, "You didn't expect that there was a woman out there so amazing." She had teased him about his "no expectation" rule, his form of self-preservation, and reminded him of the date he went on with the girl that was dirty and smelled bad after he said, "no expectations" before the date. Sarah was adamant that a no expectation mentality was a recipe for disaster and frequently teased him saying, "Make sure you don't expect your date to have good hygiene." She liked Dr. Phil's saying, "The most you get out of life is what you ask for." If you have no expectations, then you get nothing. She wasn't sure if that's how Dr. Phil intended his quote or not, but that's how she interpreted it.

Matthew was serious as he questioned, "Do you think she would date a nurse?" Sarah snapped at him, "Don't minimize what we do." Over the years, they took a lot of crap and disrespect for being "just a nurse." Especially him, being told, "Men should be doctors."

She was dreading her twelve-hour shift, but her work day was exceptionally easy as Matthew had so much extra energy that he did a lot of her charting for her. She enjoyed spending time talking with the patients sitting in the milieu playing board games as they worked on communication skills. Sarah kept telling him, "You need to call her." He would have the biggest smile, and then it would fade when doubts and insecurities crept in. Sarah had the same self-preservation conversation with him as she had with Erica. She told him bluntly, "I'm well aware of your past. She's a great woman, and you're a great man; don't forget your worth. I don't think she'll hurt you. The worst-case scenario is you end up being friends." Matthew took a deep breath and said, "I can't imagine just being her friend. I have to call her."

He drove Sarah home, and then they went into her flat where Erica had delicious homemade Mexican food waiting for them. After dinner, they played Skipbo, and then Sarah went to bed. Matthew left, but Sarah could hear them on FaceTime for the next few hours. Over the next few days, Matthew and Erica spent every minute they could together. Sarah would join them at times but was happy to have alone time to rest. When Erica had to go home, she was crying; Matthew was sad too, but he had already arranged to take a trip to Houston.

Erica and Matthew talked daily. He told her about growing up in foster care, the sports he played, and how some of his coaches were a Godsend to him. He had one great foster mom from the ages of fifteen to eighteen who helped him get his life together prior to enlisting in the Army. After a couple of years of being enlisted, he went through a nursing education program and was commissioned as a nurse. He told her it wasn't always great to work in a predominantly female environment and about how some of the nurses sexually harassed him and ones who tried to coddle and mother him. Sarah treated him like a person, a man, and then a friend. He discussed his year-long deployment to Afghanistan and what that did to him, the different moral injuries he had as the result of combat exposure, and how he dealt with it by staying busy, moving, and filling his brain with all kinds of other things as well as long distance running, talking and being in nature. He had been engaged when he left for deployment, and his fiancé cheated on him. It was more devastating for him to lose his relationship with her son than her. Traveling to different countries and having to keep his brain constantly alert with different languages, currency, cultures, transportation, and new environments prevented him from going into a deep depression.

Erica told him about the death of her father, the heartbreak she had about her marriage and the divorce from Raul, and her incredible fear that if she gave her heart away, the next man might be gay as well. That she was happy life turned out differently than she envisioned. She complained about her crazy schedule and how stressful it was to balance being a mother with a successful career, yet it was so rewarding when she got to be the first to report on a breaking news story and bring to light important issues like foster care, child abuse, animal abuse, sex trafficking, and immigration.

They talked about everything, including their future together and how they could make their relationship work. Being separated by thousands of miles was actually good because they got to know each other without sexual chemistry clouding their judgment.

Sarah teased Matthew saying, "You are a giddy little school boy, but I am genuinely happy for you, and I know you're in love." Matthew insisted on doing all of the planning for their trip to Santorini. He rented the best hotels there; he was normally thrifty, but he wanted to impress Erica. Sarah asked, "Why are you renting three rooms? Only two will be used." She had serious doubts about if she should go to Santorini or think of an excuse not to go, so they had plenty of alone time but they both wanted her there so she went. At the hotel, she was a bit lonely and wondered *am I ever going to meet somebody who is right for me? Do I have the energy to handle a relationship?*

On their third day in Santorini, Matthew insisted Sarah have dinner with them at the Athenian House, the most expensive restaurant in Santorini. The night was perfect, except Matthew was exceptionally nervous; Sarah realized he was going to propose. They tried multiple types of wine, finding the perfect one. Matthew then made a toast to Sarah saying, "I want to thank you for being the best non-biological older sister I could ever have; you're such an amazing friend, and I consider you my family. Thank you from the bottom of my heart for introducing me to Erica."

Then he looked at Erica and said, "You're amazing and have made me so happy I know we're meant to be together. I promise to be the best other stepdad to Mercedes. I couldn't imagine my life without you, and I'll do anything to make you happy; I love seeing your beautiful face, and your beautiful heart has started a fire in my soul." He then got down on one knee, and Erica screamed, "YES, YES, YES." He hadn't even asked her, "Will you marry me?" All Sarah could think was *they just met and how did he get a ring so fast without me knowing?* Yet she was happy and honored that he wanted her to share this once in a lifetime moment.

He arranged for the restaurant staff to take pictures throughout the entire dinner, planning everything down to the last detail, and God blessed them with a gorgeous ocean sunset. The evening was flawless as he destroyed every negative stereotype about how men can't be thoughtful, can't plan, or multitask. Matthew had done everything on his own. Sarah thought *this is what a man does when he loves a woman.*

5

∞

Let's Get Married

"Peer pressure plays a huge role in people's desire to get married." –Adam Levine

A Cautionary Tale

Sarah noticed Matthew's Army friend Robert at their wedding. He was hot with a well-built body. There was a lot of eye contact between them, but she didn't give him an opportunity to approach her; she was there to celebrate Matthew and Erica.

Testosterone motivates men to go after what they want and to do crazy things to get a girl. The men who asked Sarah out were more confident than the lame ones she pursued. Confidence is sexy, and she eventually lost interest in every man she pursued; they were either not interested in her or lacked initiative which usually transcended to other areas of their lives. So, Sarah found it attractive when Robert promptly contacted her after the wedding. There was definitely chemistry and she hadn't had chemistry in years. He lived a short flight from Rome in Germany and could purchase plane tickets for about €40. She cyberstalked him, and everything he had told her was legitimate.

After talking for a couple of weeks, he flew down to see her, and they went sightseeing around Rome. He was a gentleman from a traditional family with five siblings. His good manners made her lust after him even more. He frequently mentioned he was the only one in his family not married. Part of Sarah wanted to be married and share her life but only to the right person. Sharing a happy life with someone was much more important than being "married." She wasn't going to talk about marriage other than to say, "Someday I want to marry the right person."

She became sexually active at sixteen but was never promiscuous and only had a handful of lovers over twenty years of dating. She had a healthy sexual appetite even though she frequently starved it. After spending two days with Robert, the sexual chemistry took over as she ran her hands over his fit chest and biceps. She loved a man who took care of himself. They both wanted each other. It was one of those situations where there was the "I want you eye contact" followed by making out on the taxi ride home, and as soon they were in the house, the clothes were off.

Everything about his body was perfect including his stamina; she had several incredible orgasms. In between orgasms, he was affectionate and gentle as he said, "I can't wait to be married and have kids." He didn't ask her what she wanted but commented, "You would be a great mom. I bet you could easily handle five or more kids." Comments like that left her uneasy. *Did he not realize she was almost thirty-eight?* But, soon enough they were back to having amazing sex, and with sex that great, he could say anything. They spent much of the remaining visit in bed.

The passion caused her to forget how tired she was; she was awake now. Maybe this passion was what she needed. Before he left, they made arrangements to get together soon. Sarah was on a high, but also felt uneasy. She appreciated that he made an effort to visit her, but he didn't ask her many questions and wasn't interested in her rescue dogs.

Two weeks later, Sarah flew to Germany to see him. She was impressed with how clean he kept his flat; she kept thinking *he's a good guy; why do I feel uneasy?* He was classy and introduced her to his friends; they also seemed like good guys and thought highly of him. The visit included a lot more fantastic sex, and she made a conscious effort to get to know him on a deeper level asking many questions hoping that he would also want to know who she was. She asked about his interests, plans, family, friends, routines, likes/dislikes, must haves, standards, hobbies, and so on. He answered the questions with a word or two without much depth and didn't ask anything in return. She asked, "Do you want to ask me anything?" He replied, "No, I know all I need to know. You'll be a great wife and mother." Then he put his hand on her hip and started to kiss her; with a tongue in her mouth, it didn't matter that she was tongue tied. She didn't know what to say, this un-vetted assumption left her apprehensive. She tried to ignore her apprehension and not let it interfere with their time; she could talk to anybody or go sightseeing, but sex like this was rare; she wanted as much as possible before the inevitable.

They talked frequently when she returned to Italy, but she was the only one trying to have deep conversations. He often called to say, "What's up?" and that was it; she found this question quite boring. In a nonthreatening way, he made statements like "we will do this," "we will spend the holidays at," or "we will buy a house in." He wasn't forceful or controlling; he just had no insight that she might have ideas of her own to contribute to a relationship. She considered a future with him; he had good qualities, but knew she would have to live in denial if they were together. The passion would wear off; she would get used to how attractive he was and then what? As much as he talked about marriage, she was grateful he didn't propose.

After dating him for a couple of months, Sarah concluded that he's a good man and would probably be a good husband, but he was in love with the idea of being married and having a family, but he was not in love with her. He would be willing to marry anyone he was attracted to as long as he thought she fit into the life he wanted. Sarah felt sad she had to end things and would be alone again; she would miss the great sex and his fantastic body. She felt bad hurting him because he wasn't a bad guy; they just had different ideas about relationships.

He was a jerk in the breakup process and arrogantly said, "Any woman would be lucky to be with me. You're a stupid liberal woman." His actions solidified she made the right decision; if she was going to commit to forever, it had to be all or nothing. The man had to be totally in love with "her" and he couldn't imagine his life without her.

Robert wasn't the only man who wanted to marry Sarah for the wrong reasons. Years before Robert, she met Kenny online when she was thirty-four working in Korea. He was educated with an online job working from home; he looked athletic and attractive from his photos. He lived in Georgia, and she was considering moving back to the U.S.A. She loved living abroad but missed home. *Maybe there could be potential with him?*

The best thing about long distance relationships is that you get to know someone without the sexual tension and sex pheromones clouding your judgment. Kenny asked her a lot about herself, and they had honest vulnerable conversations. He told her, "My ex-wife cheated on me and got pregnant by another man; I wanted to make the marriage work even after she was pregnant with his baby, but she wanted to be with him. The worst was she had an abortion with my baby right before getting pregnant by him and keeping his baby." Sarah replied, "I'm so sorry; I feel so sad for you." She wondered *why did his wife hate him so much?* He told her, "It's important you know lying and cheating are deal breakers, and I can't go through that devastation again." He then asked, "What are your deal breakers?" She told him, "I've had a pattern of attracting men who aren't ambitious or hard-working, and they want to depend on me. I'm not sure why this happens as they repulse me. In order for me to be attracted to a man, he must be hard-working and ambitious; it's impossible for me to be attracted to a sponge. I've worked hard my entire life and done well for myself. I deserve an equal." He claimed, "I understand why these losers would be turned off; they don't deserve to be around you."

However, after that conversation, he frequently called her "sugar mama" and joked, "You make more money than me, when are we getting married? I can live with you in other countries and I will travel while you work and then come home on your days off." His idea that she would support him while he sponged off her repulsed her.

She had never met him in person, but he was consistent about communicating with her every day, and she never caught him in a lie. While it was nice to have someone consistently interested in her, he was becoming annoying. He also avoided FaceTime until she declared, "No FaceTime, no communication." He made all kinds of jokes about appearance and slammed superficial people, but she wouldn't respond until he FaceTimed her. She tried to mask her disappointment; his jokes and slams on superficial people had been a manipulation technique. He was the man in the photos, but they were taken years ago at perfect angles.

She didn't want to be superficial, and he wasn't hideous, so she continued talking to him; loneliness can cause poor judgment. The more she got to know him, the more she realized he chose to just barely get by working the minimum number of hours to support himself and didn't desire to get ahead in life. He frequently stayed at home playing video games, moved in with his parents to save money to "buy a new home" two years ago. He bragged about traveling to four countries. She had been to over sixty countries. He claimed to be an athlete but had only done one mini-triathlon.

The more she got to know him, the more she viewed him as a loser, especially when he called her a "sugar mama" despite Sarah telling him, "That's not funny; it turns me off and pisses me off." She had that unhealthy feeling if they were going to be together, she would want to change him and couldn't accept him for who he was.

After a particularly stressful nightshift dealing with psychotic and violent patients, she came home, and as she walked in the door, he was calling her. She hoped she could vent about her night, but all he did was joke about her supporting him. She went off on him, saying, "I'm not interested in you anymore. I view you as a completely asexual human, nobody I would ever have sex with. I told you I can't respect a man who is not ambitious and hard-working and all you do is make jokes about me supporting you, knowing that repulses me. You're as sexually attractive as an expired parking meter."

He fired back saying, "You're so shallow, and I can't believe you're a nurse. You must be a horrible nurse; you're so cold-hearted, incapable of caring. All I'm doing is trying to loosen you up." She thought *there's no way I can be with this idiot.* She asked him, "Do you think it would be funny if we were together and all I did was make jokes about fucking other men?" He said, "No." Still, he was clueless about why he irritated her. He tried to convince her he was ambitious, and she didn't realize it, but she wasn't easily manipulated. She hung up and blocked him from all avenues he could contact her.

Both of these relationships made her cautious of men who wanted to get married right away. Instead of thinking, W*ow, they're head over heels for me*, she thought, *what does he want from me?*

6

∞

Smoke and Mirrors, Scams and Abuse

"Some failure in life is inevitable. It is impossible to live without falling at something, unless you live so cautiously that you might as well not have lived at all – In which you case, you fail by default." –J. K. Rowling

Chrissy was Sarah's thirty-eight-year-old neighbor in Huntington Beach; she was a beautiful Filipina nurse. They ran their foster dogs together as they talked about guys. Chrissy seemed sad as she talked about being single and the difficulties finding a match. As they ran, Chrissy said, "I'm trying to get over Charlie, my ex-boyfriend, but I have so many unanswered questions. I found out he cheated on me, and I ended it without confronting him. The relationship started perfect, and we had such a good time; I cannot believe he cheated on me."

She went on to say, "We were set up on a blind date, and I went to a bar to meet him and was excited to see how handsome he was, only to find out that the guy I was talking to wasn't him but Liam. Liam and I hit it off right away, but I was there to meet Charlie. I was disappointed when he arrived; he wasn't as attractive as Liam and slightly chubby, but my friend had told me how great of a guy he was. After the first date, he walked me to my car and kissed my cheek and told me he couldn't wait to see me again. I fell for him because he was nice, interesting, well-traveled, and wooed me, not because I thought he was attractive. Liam coincidently worked with him, and we ran into him a couple of times over the first few weeks we were dating. He even whispered, "Are you sure you want to be with him?" when Charlie wasn't paying attention."

Chrissy continued the story, "Weekly he sent roses, and when I called to thank him, he would ask, "When can I pick you up for our next date?" He was romantic, and I never took advantage of him. I cooked him nice dinners and brought him food and small gifts. Everything seemed perfect." As she talked, she described red flags she had ignored. Such as, Charlie ordered her food and then asked the waitress, "Will you cut this in half? She doesn't want to eat that much." Sarah asked, "Did you want that?" Chrissy said, "No, I was still hungry; I'm an athlete; I eat." Sarah asked, "Was he ever fat?" Chrissy responded, "How did you know? He was, but lost weight to be a Navy pilot." Sarah replied, "That makes sense; what about other red flags?"

Chrissy was embarrassed as she said with a chuckle, "Well, there was one thing, but I'm too shy to talk about it." Sarah said, "Oh, come on." Chrissy said, "Okay, we had sex all the time, which was why I was shocked he cheated on me, but he could never ejaculate. One day we had sex six times, and he still couldn't get off. He kept blaming me saying I moved wrong or we were in the wrong position, going too fast or too slow. The sixth time that he couldn't finish he took his phone in the bathroom and masturbated until he concluded alone. When he came out, he had friction burns on his dick." Chrissy repeated, "I don't understand what happened." Sarah laughed, "Do you know how lucky you are to get away from him? He's a total porn addict who cannot have healthy sex with a beautiful sexy woman. He has watched so much porn and jerked off so much he can only get off with rough friction masturbation. He used to be fat and was rejected, so he's projecting his insecurities on to you. Let's hope you run into Liam again; no roses and expensive dinners are worth your self-worth." Chrissy was stunned at how fast Sarah saw him for exactly who he was.

Chrissy explained, "In the Filipino culture, if you're still single when you're in your 30s, you're an old maid or an auntie." Sarah's heart went out to her, and she suggested, "Every time somebody asks what's wrong with you, why are you still single? You should ask them, "What's wrong with you that you cannot find me a good man?"

As they stopped to let their dogs sniff, a group of young men walked by telling one guy, "Leave your wallet in the car under the seat and say you forgot it; she'll have to pay for dinner." They all seemed to think this was a good idea. Sarah rolled their eyes thinking *that is the most ridiculous advice. If he's going on a date with a girl, he might actually like her. Is making her believe he's not a responsible person a good first impression regardless of who pays for dinner?*

Ricardo was a handsome Marine who Sarah dated a few times, and then he flaked and stood her up. Six months later he called to say, "I think about you all the time; you're so beautiful, I miss you." She asked him, "What are your plans after the Marines." He replied, "I don't have many. Do you still have your nice home? Could I stay with you?" She immediately said, "I've no intention of supporting a man." He never called again.

Sarah was in two relationships in which she was the breadwinner, supporter, motivator, and mother. Her first "mothering relationship" was shortly after starting her first travel assignment in Italy when she was twenty-eight. Mason, a distant friend from college, contacted her and said, "I'm traveling through Europe. I was working for a financial company for six months, and it was bought out; all of the employees who didn't get hired with the new company received a two-year severance package. I have two years of income, and I don't have to work. I'm traveling and doing freelance photography. I would love to meet up in Italy." She said, "Sure, it will be good to see an old friend. It's exciting to live abroad, but I'm homesick with the holidays approaching."

Mason arrived in early November and stayed at a hostel. They had fun exploring Europe. He wanted to be her boyfriend, but she was not attracted to him. He stayed longer than planned, and as Thanksgiving approached, she asked, "Do you want to have dinner at my flat with some other Americans?" He said, "Yes." On Thanksgiving morning, he came over with his luggage. Dinner was nice, and everyone drank a lot of wine. Mason got drunk and fell asleep in her guest room.

The next day he fixed a broken cupboard and a leaky drain; it was nice to have him around. He reminded her, "I don't have plans after Rome; I'm taking my life day by day doing my photography business and living off my severance pay." He stayed in her guest room that night, coincidently a man broke into the flat next to hers and attempted to rob and assault her single neighbor Sofia. Sofia's screams scared him away, and he disappeared into the night.

Sofia then stayed with Sarah, and they asked Mason, "Would you please stay for a few more days?" Although Sarah had been actively involved in rescuing animals off of the street in Italy and had three foster dogs that were Pit Bull mix at that time, Mason was big and strong, a former football player, and they felt even safer with him and the dogs in the home. Feeling protected made her slightly attracted to him, and Sarah agreed to date him. She assumed Mason was selling photos as she worked. Sofia stayed until Christmas; her on again off again girlfriend visited at times. Sofia was a chef and thanked Sarah for letting her stay by buying food and cooking superb meals. She picked up after Mason, so Sarah didn't see he was a total slob. They played games as Sofia taught them Italian.

By Christmas, Sarah was introducing him as her boyfriend and glad to have a date for the Christmas and New Year's Eve parties. With the exception of Sarah frequently saying, "Clean up after yourself; I'm not your mother," things okay until after Valentine's Day. For Valentine's Day, he made her a homemade cake and bought flowers. He left a mess for her to clean, but the effort was thoughtful. He contributed to the living expenses which was nice.

After Valentine's Day, she noticed she was either nagging him to clean up after himself, to take a shower, or get out and do something more frequently. It was much easier for her to care for her rescue and foster animals than him. His diet was horrible, and he was gaining weight. She was concerned about him not having health insurance. She started to worry, *what will he do when his severance pay runs out? How will he take care of himself?* She lied to herself saying, "He must be getting money from his photography." But she felt anxious. She found cheap travel health insurance for him, and he promised he purchased it.

They continued to explore Europe, but she never developed strong feelings for him and was bored with him but comfortable. He kept gaining weight, and by March, he was seventy pounds overweight; she kept pressuring him to take care of himself. In April, he started having severe chest pains and looked like he was dying as he rolled on the floor in pain. She called 118, and the ambulance rushed him to the emergency room where they learned he had a strangulated hiatal hernia and gastroesophageal reflux disease (GERD). He had emergency surgery and Sarah was glad he had insurance. He recovered in the hospital for two days, prior to discharge the doctors had a serious talk with him about foods to avoid and lifestyle changes he must make.

As they got ready to leave, a lady from the business office stopped by and asked, “How do you intend to pay?” Sarah answered, “He has travel insurance.” The lady shook her head no, and declared, “He does not.” Sarah looked at him and asked, “What happened to that insurance you promised me you took care of?” He snapped, “Just pay it.” She was baffled he expected her to pay his medical bill. She knew she had to pay his bill if she wanted to stay in Italy with her working visa she could not have any problems. He had her listed as his sponsor in order to extend his stay, so she was loosely responsible for him. She withdrew all her savings and paid the bill.

She was so angry at him for being irresponsible, but she tried to be compassionate. He slept most of the first couple of days back; he was needy and demanding. He didn’t follow the doctors’ orders or do anything to help himself. As he slept, she wondered *what else is he hiding?* She opened his laptop and saw he had seventy-three dollars in a bank account. *Where had his two-year severance package gone?* He constantly wasted money on junk he left around the flat which irritated her as did his obsession with mindless adult cartoons. As she looked at his statements, she found all the times he said he was out doing his photography work he was actually in a pub drinking and had not sold a single photograph. She thought *how can I get rid of this loser as soon as possible?*

She searched for a cheap flight back to his parents’ house and called his mom and told her what was going on. His mom was lovely and apologized for her son. She said,

"He has been irresponsible his whole life. We hoped he would change for you; we don't know what to do."

The next day she came home from work to a huge mess but was happy to see he was gone. She walked her dogs, cleaned up and went to bed only to wake up to the hospital calling her asking her to come and pick him up. When she left for work the previous day, he drank four liters of soda knowing it was off limits which severely agitated his hiatal hernia, and he called an ambulance to take him back to the hospital. Sarah wanted to leave him there, but she was still listed as his sponsor. They were never that serious, and he was such a burden. With great resentment, she picked him up after making a cash advance on her credit card to pay his medical bills again. Johnny had convinced her to lock up all of her extra money in investments; his last bill had drained her emergency fund.

Over the next three weeks, many things prevented him from leaving, follow-up care, delayed flights, and so on. She had severe contempt towards him and resented him being in her house. He was a financial burden on her, and she flipped when she got her phone bill. He had run it up to $1,100.00. She became emotionally abusive and said things like, "How can you call yourself a man and not have a job?" "I can't wait until you leave; you disgust me; you're such a burden." As he ate, she would say "Did you pay for that?" "You're everything I never wanted in a man. I can't believe I got involved with you." "You're so irresponsible, a child not a man."

She didn't see how abusive she was, in her immature twenty-eight-year-old mind, she thought her comments might motivate him. Besides she was so angry, she didn't care how badly she hurt him. Her dad was a big enough burden; she didn't need another one.

Being around him brought out the worst in her as serious daddy issues came to the surface. She also brought out the worst in him, and he became violent, punching holes in walls shattering her belongings. He would tell her, "Shut your fucking mouth, or I'll do it for you" as he grabbed her face and squeezed it. He shoved her and bruised her up a bit.

He agreed to leave if she bought him a first-class ticket and gave him startup money. She was so desperate to get rid of him she agreed and cashed in some investments. As he flew away, she figured he cost her about $33,000.00, but a couple of weeks later maxed-out credit card bills in her name started to arrive in the mail. She was enraged and called his mother to say, "I've pressed charges."

For years after that, she vented about the loser she dated who cost her so much money. She was oblivious to how she was burdening others with her baggage. Finally, a doctor she worked with educated her saying, "The more you talk about it, the more you live it." After that, she stopped talking about how screwed over she was unless she was asked about horrible past relationships.

Her first date with Mark was going well when the bad relationships topic came up. She ranted about Mason. Mark asked, "What role did you play? If we dated, what would you say about me?" Bashing her ex was a turn off, and he ended the date with no follow up plans. The rejection hurt her ego, but she learned a valuable lesson. When you're saying bad things about an ex, you need to say. "I chose to be in a relationship with a man that…" After that when she was asked about the worst relationship she had been in she said, "He became allergic to work, and I became allergic to him." That was telling enough.

7

∞

Are You Afraid of Getting Hurt?

"I think I might be more afraid of heartbreak than of dying." –Rachel Wolchin

When Sarah was twenty-six working in Washington, D. C., she accepted a terrifying and humiliating dare from Derrick and Josh to tell Gabriel how hot she thought he was. She could feel her heart pounding out of her chest as she approached him. This was the most juvenile immature dare that she participated in since high school, and now she was supposed to be a professional. Derrick and Josh were across the gym making faces, taunting and laughing at her as she tapped him on the shoulder. Her heart beat so loudly that she didn't know what she said, but Gabriel did and had a big smile as she walked away. All she could think was *that was so humiliating, but I never have to see him again.*

At that time, Derrick was coming out of the closet, and he and Sarah would go to the gym together and have intense arguments about who was the hottest guy there. These arguments were noticeably fun and made the workouts go by faster; Josh, a heterosexual trainer, joined the debate. Derrick would come over and whisper, "The guy at three o'clock is an eight; I would totally do him" as Sarah was trying to lift weights. Gabriel was oblivious to these arguments and unfortunately oblivious to Sarah. He was focused, disciplined, and he was there to get as strong as possible. Aliens could have been working out next to him, and he would've continued to strap on heavier weights as he did pull-ups. She wasn't sure what his job was, but clearly, he had to be in great shape. Not only was he handsome, well-built, focused, and disciplined, but he was also humble; he was not like the provocative annoying men.

Sarah was never shy, and although not loud or attention seeking, she said what she needed or wanted to say. Her nervousness around Gabriel made teasing her about her crush fun for Derrick and Josh. She had wanted Gabriel to talk to her since the first time she saw him the prior year, she lacked the courage to approach him, even though every cell in her body screamed "go talk to him." This was one of the few times in her life she was afraid of getting hurt; she thought he was the most beautiful man she had ever seen and assumed he, like Caleb, was out of her league.

As the mature sophisticated professionals they were, Derrick and Josh ganged up on her and triple dogged dared her to tell him, "I think you're incredibly hot. Probably the hottest man I've ever seen." Months later as she was about to move away from Washington D.C., she accepted the dare. She was humiliated and mortified that she made a complete fool of herself as she left the gym. As she walked out, she looked back and saw that Gabriel had a huge smile. She repeated to herself, "That was so humiliating, but I never have to see him again." Her still small voice answered back, "Oh, you will see him again; you have no idea how that little act will resurface." She never forgot about the dare or Gabriel.

Some men will say, "Are you afraid of getting hurt?" as a way to manipulate women into dating them. It had worked on Sarah a couple of times but not for long.

Kelly was a fun-loving, kind hearted, single Social Worker Sarah met at a training seminar in Germany; they both were forty and became fast friends. They each had dating woes and were looking for a good match for themselves and each other. For the most part, Sarah had given up and was staying single, but Kelly was adamant Sarah go on a date with Albert, a funny, smart, ambitious younger guy who worked in her office. Sarah relented, "Okay, give him my number." Albert messaged her that night, and sure enough, he was funny and made her laugh, so she agreed to go on a date with him as long as it was something she would've wanted to do anyway; she was done wasting time and energy.

Albert stood up relieved as she arrived at a newly opened Thai restaurant. Over dinner, he told her, "Thank you for not misrepresenting yourself, so many do, and I was afraid you would be hideous." She smiled thinking, *what am I doing dating a man fifteen years younger than me?* The date was a success. Albert was a good conversationalist, but she could tell the maturity and education differences would eventually be a problem, but she was okay dating for fun and honestly looking forward to great sex. She hoped great sex with a vigorous young man could take her mind off the fact she worked for a demonic dementor and it could be a great workout, energizing her to counter her exhaustion. She hadn't had sex in two years, not since Robert.

They continued to text over the next few days. Albert was also involved with animal rescue which Sarah loved. His excessive text messages complaining about being bored were a bit annoying for a supposed ambitious guy. She thought *he should be doing something with his time besides texting me that he is bored.* She hadn't been bored in years; she was either working or pursuing goals. Albert bragged, "I'm a great cook, and I want to cook dinner for you." She had a hard day at work, and he texted her repeatedly saying, "I'm making Asian Garlic Tofu, an organic spinach strawberry salad, sweet potatoes, and tiramisu. She would tolerate his excessive texts for a dinner this amazing.

He told her his flat was hard to find, so after she reconfirmed with Kelly he was safe, she agreed to meet him in the Aldi's parking lot and then follow him to his flat. She arrived at the parking lot early and noticed a wrecked car was pulling in; it had duct tape holding the door closed. She wasn't a materialist, but she felt sorry for the person driving that car. As it continued towards her, she realized it was Albert. He pulled up and said, "I wrecked my car, but only paid $200 for this car." *That was obvious* she thought. Not only was it wrecked, but it was also filthy on the inside. As he talked to her, he put a cigarette in his mouth and took a drag. Smoking was an instant turn off; they already discussed hating cigarette smoke. So she was taken aback she made the stupid mistake of still agreeing to go to his flat.

While following him, she was kicking herself for not ditching him. She wondered *is he intentionally trying to turn me off?* As they arrived at his flat, he got out of the wrecked car; his clothes were wrinkled and dirty, and his hair was greasy and uncombed. Around the flat, the grass and weeds were three feet tall, and the odor from the flat was repugnant causing her to feel nauseous. She continued to tell herself, "Leave now!"

As they walked into the kitchen, the floor was filled with all kinds of beer, wine, and liquor bottles. He said, "Don't worry. I don't drink that much; those bottles are from my New Year's party." It was June; he hadn't cleaned in at least six months. His foster cat hadn't had a clean litter box in weeks which was evident by the waste coming out of it. He said, "I've been cleaning all day and haven't had a chance to cook." She thought *I cannot imagine how filthy the house was before he started cleaning. Why had he told me he was making dinner all day? He's a filthy liar.*

She stood at the front door and said, "I don't want to be rude, but you know that I'm a health nut and smoking is a turn off for me, so I need to go." There were so many reasons she was turned off, but this was likely the least offensive. He replied, "I'm not a smoker; my friend left the cigarettes in the car, and I was giving it a try." She obviously didn't believe him but remained polite, saying, "After I see a guy smoking, I can't imagine kissing him." He continued to try to convince her he wasn't a smoker as she looked at an ashtray full of cigarette butts next to his filthy couch. As she was walking out he became desperate telling her, "I know you're attracted to me, but afraid to get hurt." He was immature and clueless about life.

Later that night, she received several text messages reading, "Give me a chance; I know you're afraid of getting hurt. Your heart is safe with me." He was ignorant to how comprehensively repulsive and disgusting he was. Over the next week, she ignored his many messages asking, "Why?"

Sarah called Kelly and asked, "What did I do to deserve this?" Kelly apologized over and over; she had no idea how Albert was outside of work.

8

∞

The Absolutely Wrong Ones

"Because of you I'm ashamed of my life because it's empty." –Kelly Clarkson

Working in Turkey as a Nursing Case Manager was one of Sarah's best jobs. It allowed her to care for patients in a broad manner, working with the specialist and the patients to do her best to ensure they received the best comprehensive care. She believed a patient should never be treated as a disease, but as an individual with a disease who could benefit from multiple services and preventative education. Sarah talked the dieticians into collaborating with her and starting a weekly nutrition class that focused on the physical and mental benefits of a healthy gut and educating on how poor gut health impacts serotonin levels which contributes to depression.

Sarah was single her entire year in Turkey; she never met anyone she was interested in although the locals repeatedly asked her out. She was happy with her work, actively caring for the dogs on the streets finding them loving families, getting them medical care and spayed and neutered. She traveled a lot and she became friends with local women; her life was full. It took her a bit of time to get comfortable with increased affection from her female friends holding her hand when they were out walking, and the overall increase in touching and less personal space, but eventually, Sarah felt that platonic affection between friends was normal and healthy.

She was sad to leave Turkey after her year there, but she was happy to go home to Huntington Beach for a month to check on her properties and see her friends, especially Johnny and Lynn. She brought both of them all kinds of souvenirs including: Turkish delights, Nazar Boncugu The Evil Eye to ward off evil spirits, clay pottery, spices, and mini carpets. Johnny and Sarah went to tea houses and to different wineries. He advised her on the best investments and looked over her investment portfolio, and she reminded him to take time to relax and enjoy life. Lynn tried to get Sarah to go to an all-night club to meet guys, but Sarah was too tired. They went to a restaurant, and then the two of them sat at the beach talking and laughing much of the night.

After her month home, she had to fly to South Korea for her next contract position. As Tom was dropping her off at the LAX airport, he said, "I have a feeling that you're going to meet your future husband today." She punched him in the shoulder saying, "Knock it off." She and Tom had been friends for years after they met at The Tavern, a local bar where he was the head bartender. He had a good heart and was attractive with a nice body, but he was a player. She wasn't interested in players, so they remained friends. He said, "No, I'm serious; I feel it." She hugged him goodbye and put Peetee, her tiny rescued Chihuahua, in his carrying case attached to the top of her suitcase and went into the airport.

It'd been years since the embarrassing incident at the gym with Gabriel. She rarely thought of him and only told the dare story where she made a complete fool of herself to cheer someone up. She checked her bags in at the counter and entered the security line as people kept looking at Peetee and telling her how cute he was asking to pet him. He was adorable and attracted people everywhere he went. She kept looking down at him making sure he wasn't overwhelmed. As she looked up, Gabriel was standing in front of her.

Her heart stopped; he had a couple more wrinkles but looked the same as he had years ago. When her heart started back up, it raced to over 200 beats a minute feeling like a sledgehammer in her chest. Every strand of her DNA screamed, "Say something." She was standing behind him staring at him clueless as what to say. He hadn't seen her. The line moved, and people continued to approach her to see Peetee. She knew she had to say something but what? She couldn't say, "Hey, I'm that girl who humiliated myself years ago hitting on you in the gym." That would be so embarrassing. Finally, it felt like a force of nature grabbed her hand and made her tap him on the shoulder. He turned around and looked at her then smiled a huge smile showing he was happy to see her. She was thinking *God thank you for making him so handsome.* She was observant and noticed he was still in incredible shape with large muscles, but what caught her eye was he had scars across his neck that looked like he'd been cut with a knife or strangled with wires and a large keloid scar on his left bicep; perhaps a bullet or something larger grazed him. He was classy, and these scars were not likely from a street or bar fight.

Finally, she said, "I knew you from Gary's Gym in D.C." It was a total line, but all she could come up with. They both used Gary's Gym, and Gary made a point to get to know all of his customers, so perhaps he might believe this line; at least there was validity to them using the same gym. He continued to smile as he said, "Yes, a lot of us Special Operators work out there." She suspected he had some type of elite profession but was surprised he shared that information in the airport with someone he didn't know. She could tell he was also shocked that he blurted this information out. *Was he trying to impress her? Why had he done it?* With recent terrorist attacks, it was especially important for him to be covert.

She smiled saying, "I'm Sarah." He replied, "I remember your face; I'm trying to place you." She had changed her hair color and style and now dressed like a classy businesswoman not a flirty gym girl. The changes in her appearance would've made recognizing her more difficult for him. Even though he felt an incredible instant attraction to her, he immediately became paranoid thinking, *who is this woman, and why did she recognize me? Is she a terrorist or a threat?* He was sure he had met her before but couldn't connect the dots. Security called both of them to separate lines for security checks. She prayed, "God, PLEEEEEASE let him be on my flight and sit next to me." Throughout the security check then flight to Seattle, Gabriel tried to discretely look back at her trying to place her. She was aware he was studying her, but she wasn't going to say, "I'm the one who humiliated myself all those years ago." When they landed in Seattle, he waited for her to get off the plane. Sarah was so nervous she talked nonstop; her chatter eased his paranoia, but he remained guarded. This stop was a layover for her and a final stop for him. He asked her, "Will you excuse me? I'll be right back. I have to take an urgent call." The call was one of his team members letting him know there were no persons of interest on that flight.

After Gabriel came back, they continued to have small talk. It drove him crazy that he couldn't place her. He was certain he knew her; her energy was so familiar. She desperately wanted him to ask her for her contact information, but in the depths of her soul, she heard the same small voice that told her years ago say, "You will see him again." Say, "Not now, the time is not right." She glimpsed at his ticket and saw his last name was Churchill. After they said goodbye, Sarah continued on to her international flight and he to his rental car. As he placed his bag in his trunk, he realized who she was. He rushed back to try to find her, but it was too late, and he couldn't get past security anyway.

What Sarah didn't know was when she made a complete fool of herself, it was during one of the lowest points of his life. He lost friends in the line of duty, and he was dumped yet again for the amount of time and secrecy that his job required. He decided to give his full energy to his career, but he was deeply lonely and needed a confidant to talk to about all he had been through and would continue to endure with his chosen profession and a lover to comfort him. The compliment she gave him was needed and stayed with him for years. He tried to find her, but he had no idea what her name was.

Moving back to Korea was a fantastic opportunity for Sarah and she was excited about all of the cheap travel she could look forward to again. She planned to travel to every Asian country she could that she hadn't previously been to and perhaps even travel the Oceania continent. It was an overzealous goal with her unexplained pain and fatigue, but she was determined.

After arriving in Seoul, she tried to ignore her revolting gut reaction as she met her sponsor, James; he was so hideous he could make an onion cry with his mean expression, choppy red hair, sloppy clothes, jagged crooked teeth, slouched posture, scrawny limbs, pot belly, and dirty glasses that sat on the middle of his nose; his personality was even worse. He scowled and rolled his eyes as he huffed about how inconvenient it was to pick her up. She was polite and tried to have small talk as they drove to the hotel where she would stay until finding a permanent place to live. He acted like she was stupid for her questions about the local area. His social skills were lacking, and he was a smug, arrogant jerk. She didn't appreciate being disrespected, still she pitied him, as well as his wife and kids that he mentioned lived in the States; she thought *they must be glad he's so far away.*

Since he wasn't driving in the direction of her hotel, she asked, "Isn't my hotel towards the center of the city?" He huffed, "We're going to stop at Aaron's house on the way to the hotel so that you can meet the nursing team. They're all having dinner." As they arrived, it seemed more like a frat party than professionals getting together. There were six guys and three women there; three of the guys leered at her, looking her up and down. As two of the women glared at her, the third was sugary sweet. James introduced her in a territorial manner, making her uncomfortable. One of the girls muttered loud enough for Sarah to hear, "She is going to be his overseas wife." That comment was repulsive on so many levels. She wouldn't have any romance with a man she knew was committed to someone else; also he was hideous with a vile personality. She told the group, "It is nice to meet you, but I need to get to my hotel because I'm exhausted." She then walked out.

Danny was the only polite person there. He walked out with her trying to make her feel welcome as he told her about the area. It felt like she walked into some sick twilight zone. James kept her waiting outside thirty minutes as he talked to Aaron; Danny continued to wait outside with her.

She later learned that most of the nurses who she worked with were super promiscuous with each other; orgies were common, and some of the nurses were borderline sexual deviants. Fortunately, Danny was safe, and he immediately liked her.

He wanted a romantic relationship, but she wasn't attracted to him. He told her, "Our coworkers make me sick, and I secretly record Aaron; he's the alpha leader. He gets the guys together and tells them ways to manipulate women into having sex. I need protection if Aaron ever comes after me for not being 'one of the boys' or if he hurts one of the girls without her consent." He went on to say, "You remember the first night you arrived? Aaron was coaching James on how to get you to sleep with him while we waited outside. Some of the women who Aaron manipulated were Sunday school teachers, married, and been fairly moralist, but somehow he seduced them." Sarah said, "I find him sickening." Danny continued, "The leadership is charmed by him; he has gotten them laid, so it's pointless to complain. It would take an international incident for them to pretend to care. He will eventually get caught blackmailing the girls with the pictures he took of them without their consent."

It became necessary for Sarah to harshly reject James making it crystal clear nothing would ever happen with her, so he pawned her off on Aaron for the new employee check-in process. James slandered her character spreading vile rumors about her after she rejected him. Looking back, she wished she would've filed harassment charges against him at levels higher than their local superiors or gotten copies of Danny's tapes and released them to the media; there would've been outrage.

While touring around the hospital, she and Aaron stopped in the cafeteria for lunch. He was making every attempt to manipulate her into being one of his groupies. He was a sociopath, and there wasn't a chance she would be a groupies. Her decision would result in her being slandered, ostracized, and sabotaged at work. She looked away as he talked, intentionally demonstrating her lack of interest. As she looked around, her eyes locked with Calvin's eyes.

He was handsome, well-built, and looked like a badass. He was tall with short blonde hair, a square jaw, visible muscles with piercing blue eyes and a perfect smile. He sat alone a few tables over. Aaron continued to hear himself speak as Calvin and Sarah made eye contact and smiled. Aaron was completely flustered but got the hint that Sarah was not interested in him.

The next day Sarah saw Calvin in the cafeteria again and went up to him and said, "Hi, I'm Sarah, and I don't know anyone here yet. May I join you for lunch?" He was guarded, but she was an excellent conversationalist when she wanted to be. They had their first of many great conversations. Despite being a badass, he was humble and kind, and even if she wasn't attracted to him, she would've tried to get to know him because his presence was intimidating to her sociopathic coworkers. He provided her protection just by being seen with her. They tried to meet for lunch when he was there getting physical therapy for a shoulder injury. He became the bright spot in her day, week, and life. The excitement of living in and exploring new countries, putting her heart and soul into patient care, rescuing and rehabilitating animals, her faith, Peetee, and Calvin were her joys.

To decrease depression and anxiety in her patients, Sarah started group therapy outings which helped the patients socialize and feel less isolated. At first, her coworkers tried to sabotage these outings, but she convinced them the outings were a good idea by saying, "I'll take all the patients out, and you don't have to do anything. You might not have any patients to care for all day, just your own free time you get paid for." Seeing her patients get better gave her professional purpose, which was especially needed with poor peer-relationships.

She told Calvin, "I'm disgusted by the nurses I work with. They're morally sick, and I worry about the patients they take care of." Calvin respected how she cared for animals and other people. She asked him, "Do you want to help me find places to take the patients?" He liked being needed and told her, "Of course! You're always fun and different; I constantly learn from you." She also introduced him to animal rescue, and they traveled around South Korea finding homes for dogs and cats living on the streets. Sarah raised money and also gave her own money to prevent some dogs from being eaten.

Despite how accomplished he was, Calvin was deeply insecure with serious mommy issues and never viewed himself as good enough. This was a red flag, and she pretended she just wanted to be his friend, trying to deny the strong attraction she felt for him. After hanging out for about six weeks, he told her, "I've got to go back to the States in a month." This news hit her like a ton of bricks; she really liked him and depended upon his presence and company.

They increased the amount of time they spent together by running, rescuing more animals, watching movies, and exploring different areas to take her patients. The euphoria she felt being around Calvin made her forget she had felt cruddy for a long time, and she continued to grow more attached to him. Everything about him was impressive; he went to Stanford for his bachelor's degree. Then he was commissioned into the Army and was promoted early. He had been an Eagle Scout and placed nationally in both swimming and wrestling. He was a hard worker and a reliable friend. They never ran out of stuff to talk about, and he never tried to get down her pants like so many others; in fact, he never tried anything. He seemed interested, but she thought *he must be shy or his mom really messed him up when it came to women. Perhaps he is worried about a long-distance relationship and holding back is his way of self-preservation.* Intuitively, she had the strongest feeling that they would never be a couple.

The night before he was to fly back to the U.S., they went running and talked a while; she was consumed with sadness and felt like she would never see him again. They said goodbye, and she turned to leave as she fought back the tears, he said, "Sarah, wait." Then he hugged her, and finally, they passionately kissed. Then he promised, "I'll definitely be staying in touch" and kissed her a final time.

The same still small voice that she heard after making a fool of herself in front of Gabriel whispered, "You will never see Calvin again." She went home and cried herself to sleep; she had fallen hard for him. All of the crying put her in a deep sleep, and she had the strangest dream. In the dream, Calvin was just another man in a platoon of men standing in a formation as she stood about fifty feet to the side of the formation. He didn't see her as she repeatedly waved at him, hoping to get his attention. As she continued to try to get his attention, the platoon leader walked in and stood in front of the formation. She stopped waving and looked at the leader. He turned and smiled at her; it was Gabriel. He was bigger, stronger, and more powerful than Calvin, and he was the one clearly noticing her. She woke up with her heart racing.

Weeks went by, and she never heard from Calvin; she was devastated and asked around about him. Most people never knew him; out of desperation, she asked his physical therapist, "Have you heard from Calvin?" He said, "Not recently, he is on his honeymoon." She kept her emotions together until she returned home that night. When she got into the bathtub, she cried so hard her teeth chattered. *How could she have missed this?* She was humiliated and reflected back on their interactions *did he feel anything for me?* As she lay in the bathtub, the strongest impression came over her like a warm blanket, and whispered, "Calvin is not the one; there's somebody better for you. Don't forget about Gabriel."

That impression stayed with her, and she searched the internet for a Gabriel Churchill, but like Caleb, there wasn't anything about him to be found. She thought about Caleb and how he had abandoned her; she tucked that pain away for so long, but now it resurfaced. She wondered *where's Caleb? Is he married as well? Does he ever think of me? Why did he abandon me? Is this going to be a pattern in my life? Are the guys I like going to disappear with no explanation?*

She wasn't in a good place emotionally; she felt so rejected, and her snake coworkers tried to prey on her now that Calvin was gone. Different time zones made communication difficult with Lynn and Johnny; her body was in pain, and she was always exhausted and now heartbroken. Danny remained consistent in his pursuit even though she made it clear Calvin was the object of her affection. Finally, although she was still not attracted to him, she gave in. He was a nice guy, and she was vulnerable. Danny looked a lot older than he was; he was flabby and out of shape, he had lots of acne scars, and he sweated all of the time. He also stood too close and tended not to give her personal space. But he had a sweet smile, and he was safe and comfortable.

What was supposed to be a rebound relationship, turned into being with someone she didn't desire for three years. They were great travel partners and traveled around Asia and Australia. He extended his contract to match hers, and they returned to Huntington Beach together, living in her home. She tried to talk herself into loving him; but she was never proud to say, "This is my guy." They would've split up sooner with her lack of chemistry, but something always came up. He supported her through the Calvin heartbreak, and helped her get around when she fractured her ankle in Japan on one of their trips. She felt obligated to stay with him.

Four months after they returned to the States, Danny's sister, Mary, was killed in a car accident, leaving him shattered. Sarah grieved for him like she would any friend who lost a loved one. She was there for him like a dutiful robot providing connectionless sex, affection, and whatever he needed.

Three months after Mary died; Sarah was at the local health food store buying Danny his favorite food when she met Rico. As she was bending over looking at the different salads, Rico gently bumped into her and then apologized, "I'm sorry; I didn't mean to bump you. May I reach over you to grab some dressing?" Rico was really hot, and they started talking in the store and continued to talk for about an hour in the parking lot. Rico asked, "May I call you?" which reminded her Danny was waiting at home. She said, "I'm sorry, no. I have a boyfriend." Rico was forward and boldly said, "I don't think you have any passion with him, or we wouldn't have connected like this." Rico was really sexy with the body type she found so attractive; he was clean cut with dark hair and green eyes with perfect skin and teeth. He was wearing a loose tank top showing his muscular defined chest, back, shoulders, and arms. He knew she was checking him out, lusting for him. He went on to say, "This is my card; I shop here on Wednesday nights and run on the boardwalk Saturday mornings at 1000 and most evenings around 1900, and I work out at the gym across the parking lot from us."

She had always been physically and sexually faithful to Danny, but Danny could tell there was something different about her after she met Rico; she was giddy. She lied to herself, saying, "It is okay to run into Rico as long as nothing happens. I'm not calling him, and we're not having sex." They continued to run into each other a few times a week and run the boardwalk together while Danny was at home.

The sexual chemistry was powerful, and Rico knew she was struggling to stay faithful to Danny. He took advantage of her feelings and suggested they help each other stretch after they finished one of their runs. It was just getting dark out, and Rico intentionally ended their run away from the light. The stretching turned into more than a stretching session which was his intention. She hadn't been this turned on in years, and she never had an orgasm with Danny. The only orgasms she had while in a relationship with Danny were self-induced while fantasizing about other men. As they stood on the boardwalk, she faced the ocean standing by the boardwalk wall. Rico raised her left leg as she balanced on her right and placed her left calf on the boardwalk wall; he stood between her legs to "help her balance." Then he rubbed her thigh, saying, "You have tight quads that need to be massaged." He then started massaging the inside of her thigh working his hand up to her groin. She was breathing hard as she gasped, "I can't do this to Danny." As she was saying that, he was slipping his fingers under her shorts, inside her underwear and up her vagina." She was so turned on; her body was making up for three years of bad sex. He continued to stroke her clitoris as she moaned in pleasure. He taunted her saying, "Is this what you can't do? We are not kissing or fucking. I know you said I cannot do those things to you, so I'm just helping you stretch. If you want, you can come to my house or car, and I can help you stretch with my tongue. We don't have to kiss." Sarah gasped, "I can't" as he gave her an amazing orgasm with his fingers. His thin shorts revealed a large erection the entire time he was "stretching her." He then told her, "I have to get off now." He grabbed her right leg, straddling her as he grabbed her butt picking her up and sitting her on the wall. With his running shorts on, he grinded against her groin and inner thigh she was terrified people would see, but he kept going until he erupted enough to saturate his and her shorts.

After her orgasm provided a relief of sexual tension, she came to her senses and felt horrible about what she had done. Rico could care less that she felt terrible about cheating; he was happy with their orgasms, and the voyeurism was a turn on for him. She kept saying, "Oh, my God, I can't believe what I did. I can't believe I did this to Danny. I have to go; I have to clean up." Rico pointed and said, "There's a bathroom you can clean up in." He walked her to the bathroom door, and she went in and tried to make a rag out of paper towels. Rico knocked as he said, "Here, you can use my towel." She unlocked the door, and he came in locking the door behind him. He gloated, "Damn that was good. Look, I'm already hard again." As she was leaning over the sink cleaning up, he came up behind her and pulled down his shorts exposing his huge hard dick and put his hands on her hips. He gloated, "There are so many things I want to do to you. I could give you the best sex ever and make you cum so many times in so many ways." She was turned on again, but the relief from her prior orgasm left her clear headed enough to push him away as she cried, "I can't believe what I did. I've never cheated."

She planned on confessing to Danny as soon as she got home, but when she walked in, he was moving out. He was angry and bitter, intuitively knowing something had been going on. He told her, "I'm done with you." Even though she was physically present, brought him food and gifts, and said nice words to him, he never had her heart. They were no longer constantly traveling to distract her from the lack of a desire. He was growing resentful long before Rico. He yelled, "I'm leaving you; I don't want to know what's going on, and I don't care." She tried to calm him saying, "I love you as a friend; we've been through so much together." Danny shouted, "I don't want to see you, let alone be your friend. All you ever did was teach me I'm unlovable. You used me because I'm safe and comfortable, but no matter what I did for you, you could never love me." She responded, "I do love you." Danny walked out saying, "But you're not in love with me. I bet a total stranger could come along and sweep you off your feet with no effort, just a little sting from Cupid."

Seeing Danny's pain taught Sarah the importance of not getting into or staying in a relationship that her heart was not in. If she felt attracted to someone and she was in a relationship, run, avoid that attraction at all cost. She was angry at Rico but glad their encounter led to her being honest with herself about the importance of desire. She wouldn't allow herself to say "it was just a mistake" to minimize her deserved guilt. She knowingly chose multiple bad actions. The guilt she felt for hurting Danny consumed her; moments of pleasure weren't worth the acidic guilt that haunted her and stained her conscience.

9

∞

Opposites Attract? Really?

"You get in life what you have the courage to ask for." –Oprah Winfrey

Sarah looked for women to fill the void from the loss of her Grandma. She found some women she thought she thought she could connect with in her neighborhood and at churches. Consistently, they told her, "I'm worried that you're single and getting older; I want you to have a family." She assured them, "I'm fine. I like my life." They would shake their heads no and answer back, "You're not fine. Let me set you up with my…" Some setups were okay, but she was never matched with an equal. The men typically had low expectations for life. She wondered *why don't these women think I deserve an equal?*

Pam set her up with her son, "no job Rob." Pam was warm and nurturing like her Grandma, and her husband, Rob, was successful. Sarah hoped Rob, Jr. would be a catch. Over drinks, it was clear he was high as he tried to grope her. She pushed him away and asked, "Tell me about your job and interests?" He tried to gaslight her saying, "Let's talk about kitties; you're too intense." He kept responding to text messages over drinks and was so high he didn't realize she could see the texts were pictures of nude girls who were at the most eighteen. She left the date abruptly and Pam never talked to her again.

Her neighbor Debbie set her up with "not so bright Nick." They met for coffee, and he proved to be an arrogant idiot who talked nonstop. She ignored him as she waited for a good time to leave. Some of the facts he was spewing were so outlandish and inaccurate that she corrected him. He then turned red-faced, crossed his arms, and refused to speak, so she just got up and left. She called Debbie to say, "Never set me up again." In an angry tone, Debbie snapped, "I hope you didn't jeopardize my business relationship with him. Sarah had thought Debbie was odd, but now she realized Debbie was actually a lot like Nick, birds of a feather.

Pat introduced her to "emotional Oscar" and she agreed to let him pick her up and they drove downtown. As they walked down the strip, he noticed she was looking at a restaurant, so he said, "Let's go in there." She said, "It takes weeks to get reservations here." He replied, "Let's try." She was impressed he got them a seat right away. He smiled and said, "I wanted to surprise you, so I made reservations at all the restaurants in the area and watched your eyes to see which one you might like." She replied, "Wow, that's a lot of work. Thank you." On the way home, he started crying when a U2 song came on. His reaction was uncomfortable for her, and she pretended not to notice. He cried harder and said, "This music moves me. I have to pull over and listen." After caring for emotional patients daily, dealing with his emotions wasn't going to work.

She seriously wondered *do these ladies want what is best for me?* On the one hand, they would let her know that they thought she was amazing, and then on the other hand, they would criticize her for working too much, being tired, being single and not slowing down. Although she kept the good from each relationship, she distanced herself from relationships that were too critical of her life choices and her success. They were too opposite to understand her.

10

∞

Can You Learn to Fall in Love?

"I'm looking for love. Real love. Ridiculous, inconvenient, consuming, can't live without each other love." –Carrie Bradshaw from Sex in the City

Impressions or divine whispers always let Sarah know that she wouldn't be with "the one" until later in life, but she was lonely at times and wanted intimacy. Her friends and coworkers settled down and shared their lives with others. They had a partner when they were sick and to celebrate their birthday and holidays with. Sarah wanted all that.

Most of the men she dated were obviously wrong for her. When she was young and immature, she would blame the man for not being able to give her what she wanted. If she knew he was a player, she would think that she could change him, and all the red flags didn't apply to her. When her rose-colored glasses shattered, he was entirely to blame for them not living happily ever after. As she got older, she realized how ridiculous this thought process was and took responsibility for her mentality. She didn't want to change for a man; why would he want to change for her?

Her abusive father left her with an unconscious distrust of men. She was conscious of the fact that she was an independent woman and didn't need a man, but she was clueless about how her overt projection of this independence impacted men. When she would say, "I don't need you," the man would hear "You're nothing to me" or "I don't want you." It wasn't until after meeting Dawn, who was still giddy about her husband after forty years, that Sarah gained insight. Sarah asked Dawn, "How are you still so in love after forty years?" Dawn told her "I learned in my 20s to let him know I needed him, and I stroke his ego every day. This does not mean that I'm needy or dependent. It means I care about him enough to make him feel appreciated, and he goes out of his way to make me happy. I constantly build him up and tell him I'm proud of him, especially in front of people and look at the amazing life he provides." Seeing their relationship made Sarah realized how she had messed up in this area. She wondered *would the outcome of my relationships have been different if I would've told them I needed them?*

Adam was a great man, the type of friend people were lucky to have; he stuck up for the people he cared about and did what was right over what was popular. As a leader, he motivated and inspired people. He was also fun and generous. Sarah met him on a traveling assignment in Washington D.C. when he was doing an inpatient neurology consult. They were both enthusiastic about living life to the fullest. He was a brilliant Neurologist and taught her a lot; in return, she expanded his travel horizons showing him how much fun it was to go to remote places around the world.

After all of their coworkers backed out, just Sarah and Adam went on the trip to Malaysia, Myanmar, Thailand, Laos, and Cambodia. They traveled to and around the countries on planes, trains, tuk-tuks, boats, and paying random strangers to drive them. They drove motorcycles across Bagan, Myanmar to look at the hundreds of temples and rented rooms in palaces there. In the local village, they went to the same restaurant a few times. The restaurant owner was also the cook and waiter; he wore little more than underwear. Some days he charged them a dollar, and the next day it was ten dollars for the exact same food; it was hilarious. She convinced Adam to try street food and teased him for being uncomfortable when the ladyboys tried to pick him up in Bangkok.

They were great friends, and he would be a phenomenal husband if only she felt a spark, chemistry, or any desire. He asked her to marry him even though they had never kissed. She didn't mislead him; she cared about him and made it clear that they were "just friends." Every night in her room she prayed, "God please let me develop feelings for him; he's wonderful." Her friends told her, "Maybe you could learn to love him."

As they took a boat around the floating gardens in Thailand, he put his arm around her, and it would've been a good moment for her to kiss him, but she froze. Their pheromones were incompatible. She wondered *how do arrange marriages work? I don't think I could be with anyone I didn't desire.* As she was falling asleep in the hotel that night, she watched a murder mystery about a man who killed his wife because he was attracted to another woman. Of course, he was a monster, but attraction is powerful, and if it is not there, it is not there.

She cared about Adam way too much to hurt him, and after he asked her to marry him the second time, she reinforced, "You're a great man, and you, more than anyone, deserve a woman who loves and desires you with her whole heart. When you come home at night, you deserve a woman whose heart will skip a beat because she's glad to see you. You need to be with a woman who will always have stars in her eyes for you. I cannot give you what you deserve, and I value you too much to mislead you." She couldn't learn to love him no matter how much she begged God.

11

∞

Is It Really That Great?

"Wearing a mask wears you out. Faking it is fatiguing. The most exhausting activity is pretending to be what you know you are not." –Rick Warren

Sarah was a giver and keenly aware selfishness wasn't rewarded. She couldn't stand selfish people, and the only thing worse than selfish people were selfish and entitled people who never contributed to society. The wisdom and blessings she gained from her experiences being generous, combined with an open-minded mentality, hard work, and Johnny's investment advice allowed her to own an amazing home in an affluent neighborhood in Huntington Beach, CA. She loved her neighborhood because it was safe; she could run at night, and there were great restaurants and shops feet from her home. She could watch the ocean waves from her balcony. Many of her neighbors were thought leaders, movers and shakers, as well as entitled, image-obsessed neighbors.

Her most nauseating neighbor, Debbie, and her spineless, weak stock trader husband, Fred, always bragged, "We're SO RICH." Debbie was an entitled housewife who devoted her life to an image. From a distance, Debbie and Fred made their lives look like everything was "SO GREAT," and they looked like an attractive couple; up close they looked like plastic surgery junkies. They drove Porsches, bragged about their luxury vacations, spa appointments, country club and yacht club memberships. They wore flashy provocative clothes and jewelry. Ideally, Debbie should've been able to relax and enjoy life but she was miserable and complained relentlessly.

Sarah's intuition came from an innate ability, childhood experiences, and her work that required her to size people up. She instantly knew Debbie and Fred were frauds. They caused so much conflict in the neighborhood with their entitled demands. Sarah had to "cat them." Her foster failure cat Henry taught her only to acknowledge the things that are of extreme interest or value and blatantly ignore everything else including her when he felt like it. Debbie and Fred had no value to add to her life, so it was easy for her to "cat them," but seeing how they treated the maintenance people and how they bullied Clarice and William, an elderly couple who selflessly served on the association and generously paid for the neighborhood improvements with their own money, left Sarah enraged. They accused Clarice and William of embezzling association funds and demanded they manage the association's dues. This request didn't go over well as most neighbors detested them.

It took every ounce of energy for Sarah not to rip them apart. She always tried to use her exceptional knowledge of human behavior to restore individuals, but she had the ability to shatter an ego if she wanted. She knew if she ever unleashed on Debbie, Debbie would likely never recover from the damaging verbal blows. Sarah restrained from telling her, "You're a disgusting role model for your three daughters, teaching them to be materialistic, image-obsessed, lying, mean-spirited women, completely dependent on a man. You have no independent value, and I see through you. Your daughters will have a messed up mentality requiring years of therapy."

Instead of giving them the reality feedback they needed, she used her energy to support Clarice and William to let them know how appreciated they were. She cooked dinner and had them and her neighbors Jewel and Jewel's husband Jerry over for dinner. When Jewel arrived, she announced, "Debbie and Fred are moving. I know we are all ecstatic; the tension will now go away." Jerry chimed in, "Oh, they're buying a big fancy house a few streets over." Jerry was friendly and well spoken, but Sarah wondered what he was thinking most of the time. He wasn't the sharpest. Sarah said, "I don't believe that; there's no way they could afford another home here. The market's not doing well, and brokers are losing their jobs; something's not right."

She got on her laptop, and within a couple of minutes had the property records of the homes that they supposedly owned. They were short selling their current home before it went into foreclosure, and the house they were supposedly buying was a rental. Jewel said, "I figured. Is there anything else to this story? What else are they doing to maintain their delusional image?" When Fred was arrested for embezzlement shortly after he and Debbie moved, Sarah thought *karma's a bitch; no wonder he wanted the association dues.* He was sentenced to five years in prison, and Debbie was on the hunt for her next rich husband days after he was locked up. She wasn't going to work.

Sarah told Jewel, "For the people who never think about depth, Fred and Debbie would've seemed like the "perfect couple," but it was a facade. I'm so grateful to be comfortable being exactly who I am, even with my flaws. I'm grateful for my real friendships with you, Clarice, and William. I prefer authenticity to the perfect image."

And NO, it wasn't that great as Fred sat in jail, and Debbie had to get a job because her next two husbands were also con artists.

12

∞

Almost the Right One

"How do you love someone and just... Walk away? Just like that. You just, go on as normal... You get up, get dressed, go to work... How can you do that? How can you be okay with that?" –Ranata Suzuki

From age thirty-five to thirty-seven, Sarah was back working in the States. She was glad to be home and back with "her family" also known as Johnny and Lynn. She signed a yearlong contract to work on the Psychiatric Inpatient Unit at the Huntington Beach Hospital. Inpatient nursing was where she cared for people at their most vulnerable and where she learned the most about what people need. That was where she was able to have an impact on their lives, as she had done with Raul. She motivated people with her emotional strength when they were at rock bottom and loved seeing their mental health improve. Between the litigiousness that goes along with mental health care and a lack of gratitude that can come with an unhealthy mentality, mental health nurses rarely get the thanks they deserve. Her biggest reward was feeling confident patients wouldn't commit suicide after she cared for them.

Newly hired staff sat waiting for the Chief Executive Officer (CEO) to come in and tell them his expectations, the vision for the hospital, and so on as part of their orientation. She heard the whispers, “I heard this CEO is a real jerk.” After waiting a few minutes, a young-looking, handsome man walked in and started talking to the group. She didn’t hear him introduce himself, but the moment she saw him, he had her attention. He was impeccably dressed, well spoken, clearly intelligent, and confident with the physique she found so appealing. As he talked, she leaned over to the man sitting beside her and asked, “Who’s this?” He replied, “Justin Jones, the CEO.” *It can’t be. He’s way too young,* she thought. He looked to be about thirty-five. During his talk, he seemed to keep looking at Sarah, but she assumed it was her imagination. At lunch, she almost dropped her lunch tray on the cafeteria floor as she turned around, and he was standing right behind her waiting to introduce himself. There was a magnetic chemistry.

Over the next few weeks, they seemed to run into each other everywhere. Her coworkers teased her saying, “He has never visited the ward and now makes excuses to visit every shift you work. He’s single. Maybe if you gave him some good loving, he might stop being a jerk and give us a raise.” Her wages were set by the contract company not by the hospital so he had no direct impact on her pay.

He invited the mental health team to hospital functions and social events and started discussing the importance of mental health care during his interviews. Her coworkers continued to insist the additional attention was because he liked her. She didn’t see it until she saw the hospital Christmas party photos. She had been playful at the Christmas party and went around taking pictures with different people. Women threw themselves at Justin, but he didn’t notice them as he was focused on her. Eventually, she walked over to him, and the five women trying to get his attention seemed to go away. He grabbed her and kissed her and said, “I want to date you.” This forward act was a bit much; they had only previously interacted through smiles, eye contact, greetings, and causal short professional chats. He was drunk, and some of the Directors were nearby, so she said, "Merry Christmas, Justin." Then walked away thinking *I can't believe that he kissed me, there must be a rule against the CEO dating employees.*

Later that night she asked her friend Diana, a renowned radiologist that worked at the same hospital, "Do you think he wants to date me or was that drunk talk?" Diana replied, "I'm sure he wants to date you. If it was drunk talk, why not ask any of the women throwing themselves at him?" They sat down and looked at the photos of the evening. In many of the photos, he was in the background of the pictures looking at her with a big smile. Diana laughed, "Well, that settles it."

The following Monday, he found her in the hospital cafeteria and said, "It's my birthday Thursday, and my friends are throwing me a party. I want you to be my date." Several staff members were staring at them. She found his persistence attractive but didn't want the "sleeping with the boss reputation," and even though she wouldn't admit it, the low self-esteem side of her thought I'm not worthy of a man like this; he's out of my league. When she had these thoughts, she reminded herself I'm smart, kind to animals and most people, educated, well-traveled, financially secure, beautiful, I take care of myself, and I have good morals. So, who are these women that are better than me? She smiled as she said, "I don't want to get you into trouble."

Later that day he emailed her an invitation to the party, and his secretary, Ruth, came to the ward where she was working with the address and directions to the party. Ruth smiled and said, "You should know, he is shy, but he likes you a lot. I think you should go to this party. Do you want me to send transportation for you?" Sarah said, "No,

I can drive myself, but thank you." Sarah repeatedly heard that he was a confirmed bachelor and wondered *is he a player?*

She put on a sexy purple dress showing her large cleavage and accenting her curves for the party and bought a certificate for twenty dog beds at a local shelter in Justin's name as a gift. She gave him the certificate and a bottle of wine with a hug and kiss on the cheek as she arrived. It was his forty-sixth birthday, but he looked ten years younger. He didn't keep it light and doted on her as he got quite drunk again which was concerning. With drunk courage, he proclaimed, "I've been attracted to you since the first moment I saw you." She asked, "Aren't you concerned about what the directors think?" He sneered, "No, you're a contractor. You don't work for me, and I'll fire them if they piss me off." She wasn't sure if his arrogance was appealing or just plain egotistical.

After the party ended, he walked her out; the chemistry was intense, and they couldn't stop kissing. He told her, "I can't wait to see you again" and wouldn't let her go until a date was confirmed for the next night. She was on cloud nine; mutual attraction with a man this persistent and successful was extremely rare.

She had the next day off; twelve-hour shifts gave her three to four days off every week. He called the first thing in the morning to tell her, "I had a great time with you last night and want to see you tonight. You can come up with something for us to do, and I'll pay for it." Roses and lilies arrived before she had even showered with a note that read, "From Justin." Prior to leaving the hospital, he called and asked, "What did you come up with for us to do?" She answered, "There's a great Italian restaurant with dancing." "Great, what's the address? He asked, "I'm on the way to pick you up." As he opened the car door for her, she saw he had directions to the restaurant printed with two parking garages circled and the address plugged into the GPS. He got in the driver's side and leaned over and kissed her, ensuring she knew they were not going to be "just friends."

The food was delicious; the wine, bread, oils and music and ambiance made the night extra romantic. They danced and kissed; the sexual chemistry was insane. She really wanted to sleep with him and was sure he was going to try that night; she could feel his interest when they danced close. After dinner, he drove her home, kissed her goodnight at the door, and then made sure she got in the house before he left. This was not what she expected.

They went out for several more dates over the next few weeks. He always had her plan the dates; he wasn't good at making plans for fun. After the dates, they would kiss and have serious foreplay for hours at her home before he would leave. It was driving her crazy. *Why isn't he trying to sleep with me?* She thought. On the evenings that they didn't go out for a date, they went running or to the gym. The euphoria of falling in love and extra exercise caused the pain that she was in over the past few years to be almost unnoticeable.

After a few weeks of dating, she was all over him. They had been on several dates, and she was concerned he might not want her as much as she wanted him. She told him, "I want you so bad, and I can't wait any longer." He said, "I feel the same. Let me go to the store and get condoms." As soon as he got back, she was all over him again. He kissed her gently and said, "Not like this, let's take it slow. I want us both to be completely comfortable." She felt rejected. *Why did he not feel comfortable?* But then he took his clothes off down to his underwear, and he was completely erect as he said, "I care about you, and I want this relationship to work. I want to sleep with you all the time and for us to be completely comfortable, not rush into anything. How about if we sleep next to each other and make sure we are compatible sleeping together?"

They tried their best to sleep, but the repeated foreplay interrupted the sleep. When the sun came through the next morning, he looked at her and said, "I can't wait any longer." She replied, "Me neither." He put his perfect penis inside her and started to make love to her as she squealed with pleasure. He had great moves and thrust her over and over again until she screamed as she had one of the best orgasms of her life. He smiled and asked, "Was that good for you?" "You have no idea," she panted. He replied, "Do you mind if I go a little longer?" She responded, "Please, I want you to feel as good as I do." It felt fantastic to have him inside of her as he lasted for a couple more minutes and then he seemed to be as satisfied as her. He then held her saying, "You have no idea how much I care about you." They cuddled with her head on his chest as Peetee scratched the bed to get up with them. Justin picked him up, and Peetee cuddled between them. Everything seemed to fit. Less than an hour later they were making love again and then one more time after that. He didn't want to leave but had a lot of errands. Before he left, he asked, "Do you and Peetee want to come over for dinner?" "Of course, I want to spend all the time I can with you," she replied.

It was her first time at his house. When Sarah arrived, Justin was in the kitchen cooking with a special plate prepared for Peetee. They immediately started kissing. Then he stopped them laughing, "The dinner is burning, make yourself at home." She walked around the house and noticed he was obsessively clean and organized. After dinner, they sat on the couch, and he turned on the TV to watch a basketball game. He was oblivious to her lack of interest in the game, but she did enjoy cuddling up next to him. After a few minutes, it didn't matter what they were watching. They gave into passion again and again; they were as sexually energetic as horny teenagers. Their sex life continued to get more amazing over time. Every time they both had a day off, they had morning sex at least three times.

They fit together; dating was easy and natural. His incredible ambition was driven by bad anxiety, and she helped him relax and have fun. She wondered *will he care about me enough to give up his commitment to being a confirmed bachelor?* He had to have routine and structure in his life, which usually benefitted her. After making love on the Saturday mornings she didn't work, she would often fall back to sleep, and he would get up and organize her already clean home then take their cars to be cleaned or in for maintenance. They were busy yet still made as much time as possible for each other.

After dating a few months, he asked "Do you want to live with me? You can have extra money by renting your home. You don't have to pay for anything here." She was nervous about moving in; it was a big step, but she loved him and wanted to be with him as much as possible. After living together for a few months, she leased her home. He continued to make her life easy. He found recipes for gourmet dishes that they cooked together. He wasn't possessive or jealous and glad to have her friends over for dinner. He didn't complain when she was out with friends, and he gave her plenty of space. He loved Peetee and played with him as soon as he got home. Some of her friends liked him, and others pointed out that he was demanding, emotionally selfish, and everything had to be his way. Occasionally, she noticed small things; they only watched what he wanted on TV, and he would never take a vacation or travel for fun with her. If she wanted the two of them to go to something he wasn't interested in, he would not go.

The hospital staff told her, “He’s more pleasant to work with and not micromanaging us as much.” He rushed home after work to be with her, and she had no doubt that he loved her even if he had a hard time saying it, his actions did. He often cooked her lunch for the week. They took walks around his neighborhood. His neighbor who had dementia introduced herself to them every time she saw them. Sarah would introduce Justin to her by saying, “He is my houseboy.” But she was proud to say to others, “My boyfriend is smart, ambitious, hot, a helpmate, and he makes my life easy.”

He no longer wanted to be a confirmed bachelor and started bringing up marriage. He asked, “If we got married, would you agree to sign a prenuptial agreement saying that we would never have kids? Not biological, foster, or adopted, no kids at all. That would be the only thing I want. If we got a divorce, you could take me to the cleaners and take all my money. Just no kids.” She responded, “No, I’ve always seen myself as a mother; the time just hasn’t been right.” They argued or changed the subject when this topic came up for months. At times, he would become distant and unaffectionate pushing her away but then be loving and tender other times. He loved her, but his push-pull was hard on her. He would tell her, “I can’t have kids because of my mother. I’ll never bring a child into the world to suffer like I did.” When he told her about his childhood abuse, it wasn’t nearly as bad as she and her patients experienced, so she didn’t buy this excuse. She did agree that his anxiety made it hard for him to have kids, but much of the reason that he was so successful so young was driven by his anxiety and his way to prove his ridiculously critical mother wrong.

Sarah’s contract was about to be up, and she had to decide what she was going to do. She could extend the contract, find another local job, or take a traveling assignment.

Her home was rented, so she could not go there. The fighting about not having kids was becoming too much for her. She loved him and wasn't ready for it to be over, but they needed to reach an agreement. She would ask, "What are we going to do?" He couldn't deal with the possibility of losing her, yet he wouldn't give her what she wanted, so he kept avoiding the conversation.

He was deep into self-preservation, pushing her away by acting like a jerk and numbing himself with extra work and alcohol. Finally, she cornered him and asked, "I need to know if you'll give me what I want? It does not have to be now, and we can take our time so that you won't be so anxious, but I won't give up being a mother." He had a mild panic attack and began to feel faint, his heart raced, and he started sweating. He kept saying, "I care about you, but I can't have kids." Then he walked out. She sat in the shower crying for hours as the water washed the tears away.

She knew what she had to do and contacted the travel nursing company she had worked for to let them know she was available for a New York City assignment as long as they provided pet-friendly living. She was glad to move; he had been acting like a jerk to hide his pain and living with a jerk was not fun.

After she left, he worked constantly to fill the void she left. After a few weeks, he missed her so much he couldn't fight his urge not to call her. He called her on a Saturday morning which would have been the time they would normally be making love. He talked about a bunch of random stuff that didn't matter like how many miles were on his Land Rover and so on. Finally, he told her, "I miss you and need you to stop my pain." She missed him too, and they started to talk again. She lied to herself saying, "Communication won't hurt because we are not together, and there is a distance between us." She was in denial, and these chats caused her to want him back desperately; she was living in a fantasy and denying reality.

In between his calls, her neighbor committed suicide. She told Justin, "I can't believe I missed the signs. He was friendly when we talked in the elevator. It's my job to recognize the signs; how did I miss this? He replied, "Well, my day was worse; try running a hospital." The distance allowed her to clearly see his selfishness. He was also not empathetic to how bad her exhaustion and pain was getting. Lynn had the needed come to Jesus talk with her reminding her, "You always talked about being a mother, and if you give that up for a man, maybe I don't know you." This talk was the wakeup call she needed. She firmly told Justin, "If you don't want to give me what I want, stay out of my life." They stop communicating after that; he had never once offered to come to NYC to see her. She was heartbroken; it was the first time in her life she had been with her "almost soulmate." For months she felt like a zombie, just surviving life.

She needed time to heal and didn't rebound like before or even pretend to. Her heartbreak felt like her foundation was ripped out from underneath her. She questioned God asking, "Why did you bring him into my life, let us have such joy, and then rip us apart?" She thought *surely it was God's plan that we were together because Justin needed to see what real love was like*; years later she could see the relationship raised her standards.

After about a year and a half of not being able to let him go, she went to China to run the Great Wall of China marathon, fulfilling a bucket list goal. She was only able to do the half marathon because of her pain level, and she was too tired to care that she only partially met her goal. While she was there, she met two amazing men also trying to get over broken hearts. They were attractive, ambitious, professional men. George was from England, and Andrew was from Romania. George told her, "I'm trying to run out the pain. If my physical pain is as bad as my emotional pain, then I'm balanced." After a weekend hanging out with these men, she pondered *why am I still hung up on Justin when there are amazing men like this out there?* After China, she declared to Diana, "I'm over Justin; the chemistry is dead." Diana insisted, "I don't think this story is over. Justin will be back in another chapter." Sarah didn't agree.

After China, she took a job as a prison nurse. Her boss, Leann, was one of the best advisors and mentors she had ever worked with, and Sarah loved to come to work. Leann brought out the best in the people. She was generous and made a big deal out of each employee's birthday. Leann led with enough guidance that she ensured the standards were met but gave her employees the freedom to grow professionally. The medical benefits were excellent, and Sarah went to her primary care doctor frequently, mainly for exhaustion, pelvic pain, and total body pains, even her knuckles hurt. She knew something was wrong, but nothing could be found on the diagnostic tests.

Aden was a Major in charge of the correctional officers, and Sarah coordinated patient care with him. They clicked right away; he was polite, professional, exceptionally intelligent, and handsome. He talked about his strong Christian faith, morals, and values openly. These qualities had become more important to her as she got older. He invited her to game night and to church. She wasn't sure if it was a date or if they were just friends. She respected him, but she was not sure if she was attracted to him. If he was attracted to her, he was holding back. They ate lunch together at work, and he continued to invite her out to do "group things." She found out he had recently gotten a divorce after his wife cheated on him in the worst possible way.

Aden was kind, humble, and generous. He was a good friend to a lot of people. He had been successful in his career, but his family came first, the exact opposite of Justin. Aden's interest in flying reminded her of Caleb. He rented a twin-engine plane and took her and others flying. She was proud to know him and questioned, *am I attracted to him?*

Sarah saw nonviolent patients with no history of sex crimes in her office. If patients were convicted of sex or violent crimes, she talked to them in a cell with a glass wall between them or with a guard present. She didn't look at the patients' criminal records prior to seeing them. That Monday she noticed Aden walking by as he was giving training to a group of new hires down the hall from her office. They waived as she took a patient into her office.

After she closed the door, she had a bad feeling in her gut about the patient, but she maintained her composure trusting that the guards had properly screened the inmates. The patient had very long fingernails and kept rambling about vague symptoms and not reporting anything concerning or abnormal. As he kept rambling, she noticed a paper from his criminal file was misplaced in his medical record. This was an odd mistake. She froze and tried to act like she was still listening to him as she read, "sexually violent predator." She looked at her door to see if anybody was walking by her window with an incredible uneasy feeling, knowing this inmate's file was accidentally placed in the wrong section.

The inmate knew something was wrong. She looked at him and quickly said, "I think we're done; I can't find anything wrong with your health. I think you're having normal stress for a prison environment. I'm going to get the guard to take you back to the holding area." The inmate reached across the desk and grabbed her throat as he climbed across the desk and sneered, "Bitch, you're going to give me some pussy." She screamed until he squeezed hard enough to clamp her vocal cords shut; she struggled to pull away from him as his nails cut into her neck, leaving her bleeding. By the grace of God, Aden heard her screams and got to her office tossing the inmate off her. After the inmate was locked up in isolation, Aden came back to check on her.

She was frozen in fear and numb with shock. He put his arm around her and wiped the blood off her neck as he whispered, "You're alright. It's okay. I'm here. You're safe." He repeated this assurance as he cleaned her up. Leann ran to her office when she heard, uttering, "Are you okay? I'm so sorry." Leann was so supportive.

Aden took Sarah home and then told her, "I can stay in your guest room." She was still terrified, and he was a needed comfort. After he cooked dinner, they played cards. She kept thinking *he's my knight in shining armor. Men like him don't exist; he's everything a girl could want. Do I want him?* He stayed in her guest room until she became comfortable being alone again. They were great friends, and she admired, respected, and cared about him tremendously. She wondered *does he care about me as more than a friend? I'm too afraid to ask, and he's a traditional guy, so he wouldn't appreciate a girl making the first move. What if he never wants to take the friendship to the next level? Is he afraid because of his ex-wife?*

She eventually realized there was a lot of benefit that came out of her relationships with both Justin and Aden. Justin taught her what it was like to be with a helpmate and an amazing lover, somebody who was ambitious and shared the responsibilities. He proved strong mutual magnetic attraction was not just in the movies. After Justin, she was quick to walk away from a guy saying, "Nope, I know what it is like to be with someone who enriches my life, and that is not you." Aden was the example of a great man like she had never seen before. Justin set the standard on how a relationship should be, and Aden set the standard on how a man should be.

Years after she and Justin broke up and Sarah was in remission from the cancer that almost killed her. Justin learned she was back home. Out of the blue, she opened up her door and was surprised to see him standing there. Her heart didn't skip a beat as it had before, seeing him was like seeing an old friend. She had let her heart properly heal and had not tried to numb the pain with other men or sex. She was truly over him. She had gratitude that he had been in her life and for what she learned from him. He hadn't gotten over her; he tried to compartmentalize his pain and forget about her, but that didn't work. She gave him a hug and invited him in for a visit. He was having a hard time talking, so she told him about how sad she was when Peetee died of unexpected heart failure, and how she finally got properly diagnosed which explained why she had been fatigued and always in pain. How she almost died a few times but was doing great now.

Since their breakup, she had traveled to several different countries, ran the Great Wall of China half Marathon, went to Africa for a safari and ran the Big Five Marathon with zebras, elephants, and giraffes. Then she went to Greenland and ran the Polar Circle marathon and ran through the Petra desert in Jordan.

As she talked, she thought, *wow my life is amazing; I'm so glad things didn't work out with Justin.* Ironically, during her second surgery, she learned her uterus was inhospitable and could have never hosted a baby. Her desire to have a baby was the biggest reason for the breakup. If she would have known that when they were together, she might have reconsidered having kids. She smiled as she thought *God's timing is perfect.*

13

∞

Maybe There's Nothing Wrong with Me; If I Wanted to be Married, I Would

"What's meant to be will always find a way." –Trisha Yearwood

Many people are so desperate to get married that they get married, and love and compatibility are not necessarily part of the equation. A few years later, many are miserable with their loss of freedom, personal space, time, friends, hobbies, and goals because they're married. The stress of marriage shows in a lack of self-care and extra weight but is most transparent in their attitude.

Sarah believed that about 20-30 percent of the marriages that didn't end in divorce were actually good relationships, but only 10 percent were really happy, the type of relationship she wanted. She was more fearful of losing her freedom than heartbreak. She was an insomniac. W*hat if he snored? Or worse, hit the snooze button? What if he stopped working and sponged off me or he ran me into financial ruin after I've worked so hard? What if he couldn't make a decision; I can't stand wasting time? What if he drank the last of the milk, and I don't have any for my morning coffee? What if he wanted to come on my annual girls' trip? What if he talked nonstop after I listened to patients all day? What if he was a slob or turned into an adult child? What if he was more work than he was worth, and I was already married to him? My energy level is dropping; I can't* *take on more work.* These thoughts ran through Sarah's mind. She took single life for granted until her patients and friends confided their marital woes to her.

Her relationship with Danny was one of the experiences that cleared up the false belief that attraction must be sacrificed for a "good heart." After settling and being miserable with a few guys, Sarah learned she was attracted to people for a reason; her desires came from somewhere and could not be forced. If she was going to date or marry someone she was not attracted to, she was going to hurt them much worse than if she rejected them. Sarah knew that feeling undesired is a horrible feeling.

She strongly believed that we are pieces of life's puzzle, and we cannot see what God's plan is until the puzzle comes together. Countless times she stayed late at work to care for high-risk suicidal patients knowing she was exactly where she was meant to be. If she had a husband, she would have to choose between going home to her husband or taking care of the patient.

Sarah valued relationships tremendously, and if she had been with her soulmate early, she wouldn't have appreciated the importance of her time and attention. It was God's plan she would eventually contribute to the world touching lives on a global scale which would take tremendous time and energy. Her soulmate needed time to grow into a man confident enough to be with a woman like her.

14

∞

Dear Past Me,....Love, Future Me

"Maybe I don't have to know what my fate is to know that everything will be okay... Wherever I'm headed, I know it's exactly where I'm supposed to be." –Susane Colasanti

Life is a puzzle with pieces coming together when they should. Sarah wondered *what does my future hold? So much of my life has not turned out how I expected. I thought for sure I would've gotten married and had a family by thirty. I've made the most out of life and took every opportunity that has come my way, but I'm lonely. Why have I never found a partner to share life with, a helpmate, someone to make life easier? Am I ever going to have a family, or do I have to stay single to fulfill my life's purpose, whatever that is? That's not what I want, but it doesn't seem like there's anyone on the horizon; look at the number of bad dates and relationships I've gotten myself into.* Life was testing Sarah to see if she had the strength to handle it. Experience taught her that life was so much more than "me," and she was on this planet to serve and care for others.

During these periods of depression, she did serious soul-searching, often looking up videos on YouTube and surfing the internet on different topics. She used keywords and phrases such as life's purpose, meaning, faith, hope, healthy relationships, soulmates, destiny, meant to be, God's plan, and so on. She came across videos of people she deeply admired reading letters they had written to their younger selves.

These letters inspired her, and she watched and read all she could find. Time and time again, the advice that was given was "Relax; it will be okay. Life works out the way it should. Trust your intuition." She could see this work for others but not always for herself. She knew she shouldn't, but she struggled with doubt. Many times, she was scared, anxious, and filled with discouragement and didn't think she could handle the challenges she faced, but she worked hard, and fate stepped in. Later she would look back and think *that wasn't that hard.* This pattern would then repeat with the next challenge she faced.

She prayed relentlessly to God that different relationships would work, and later she would be so grateful they didn't work for so many reasons. The biggest reason, although she didn't know it at the time, was because she was destined for greatness, and if a relationship worked, she would not have fulfilled her destiny. After weeks of researching these letters, she had a powerful dream. In the dream, her sixty-year-old self was writing to her forty-year-old self. The dream went like this:

Dear Past Me,

I'm writing you this letter to say, "I'm sorry that your heart is hurting right now and that you're lonely; know you are so loved. I loved you then, but I love you so much more now, and take better care of you. I especially protect and guard your heart, and we don't suffer unnecessarily as much as we used to.

You're meant to live a big life, and trust me, we live an extraordinary life, so much more than you could have ever envisioned. But, to live a big extraordinary life requires growth, and we grow in our pain. So, what I need to let you know is you're going to go through incredible pain that you could have never predicted. This pain will change us and cause us to grow becoming the person we are today. Our priorities and goals will change in ways you could have never imagined. You will have to let go of dreams and desires you had your entire life, but they will eventually be replaced with more than what you could have ever dreamed or desired. Knowing that you're creating a legacy of making changes for the better in the world and touching others on a global level will be one of your greatest joys.

It's important that you have a premonition something bad is going to happen so that it won't break you. You will soon face incredible pain. In the depths of your pain, your friends, who you thought would love and support you, will betray you in ways you could never imagine showing you how astonishingly selfish they are, adding to your pain when you're already so broken. They will invalidate your suffering and make you feel like you're weak and crazy. You will be in such a low place when this betrayal happens that to survive you will have to eliminate these "friends" from your life. All of that is God's plan; he had to do a clearing in your life you were not willing to do on your own. You thought because you had been friends and soul sisters, shared years of history, laughs, heartbreaks, struggles, and so much fun that they were meant to be in your life. The truth is they were holding you back and draining your energy. The relationships were always imbalanced, you always gave more, and your cup wasn't being filled. You will be amazed at the friends who step in and will love and support you when you are at your rock-bottom.

You needed to suffer to develop a compassion for yourself so that you would stop allowing yourself to be used. You have always cared deeply for others, but the pain you will face will deepen your character and expand your ability to be even more compassionate.

Encouragement and support from those who want the best for you will help propel you to the next level again and again; levels where your passion for helping others have profound impacts around the world, not just with your patients. You will be even more outspoken and supportive of others but from a much bigger platform. You will reach people you will never meet. Your destiny is to leave your mark on this world.

In the process of becoming the amazing woman we are today, you will have to develop a confidence and strength in yourself you didn't know was lacking; rising above the pain when you feel so weak and helpless is where your strength will come from. You will learn to relate to and feel for people and circumstances in their rock-bottom that you never could have if you hadn't been there yourself. The suffering you will go through is what causes you to develop a kindness that people recognize and are drawn to.

Doubt and discouragement are your Achilles' heel. Many times, you will give up your joy for anxiety and stress trying to force something to happen that was never meant to be. You will continue to struggle, but your faith is stronger than any doubt and discouragement. You will learn there's a time and place for vulnerability, especially when it comes to romance.

You're probably wondering why I have not brought up romance yet as that is what you spend so much of your time obsessing over. The amount of time and energy you're wasting is actually quite annoying. When you're at rock-bottom, you will have no choice but to take care of and love yourself completely if you're going to rise again. By that, I mean COMPLETELY. You will only allow the light in, and this becomes true for all areas of your life. When you come out of this prolonged season of testing, suffering, and character development, you will know you can only be with a man who is the same caliber as you. Someone you're going to grow with and bring out the best in each other supporting each other's dreams, goals, and autonomy. You will be partners on every level. Don't worry; you will have incredible chemistry and attraction, and you don't have to sacrifice that. I know sometimes you think if you get a man with heart and character, you will not be attracted to him. Don't worry; he's very hot. You have to be with a man of excellence, someone you're proud to be with, or it will not work. You're not meant to share your life with this man when you're young as you both have to have your own journey of self-discovery. Neither one of you would become the person you are meant to be if you didn't walk alone, make mistakes, and grow from those mistakes.

I would love to tell you to stop this crazy dating and wasting your time with all of the wrong men and focus on how amazing life is. I would love to tell you to put that energy into something productive, but to change one thing is to change everything, and we don't want that. So, go ahead and keep making mistakes; I understand we are designed to need a companion. Have compassion for yourself, hit rock-bottom, fall down, and get back up again and again. Have faith that everything will work out better than you can conceive. Remember you're so loved!

Love,

Future Me

P.S. Remember that Oprah said, "Few regrets means a life well lived."

The dream transitioned, and Sarah was sitting across from her Grandma at her Grandma's kitchen table. Her Grandma was drinking coffee and smiling at her. There was such an intense and consuming feeling of love. Then her Grandma said, "My life stopped, Honey, yours didn't. It's time for you to get to work." Sarah abruptly woke up confused with so many mixed emotions.

15

∞

How It Should Be

"Real love moves freely in both directions. Don't waste your time on anything else."

–Cheryl Strayed

There are many competing theories about the purpose and meaning of dreams. Are they a preview of coming attractions? A premonition? Windows into the unconscious? A message from a guardian angel or God? Is the brain simply unwinding or sorting out thoughts? Are dreams even relevant? Sarah wasn't sure what her dream meant, but she felt it had a profound meaning, and she refocused on how she looked at love. What does love look like? Is there a standard for love?

She was numbing out on TV watching Oprah interview a famous singer talking about how she will always love her abuser. She was one of the most talented and beautiful singers in the world with millions of fans. Sarah thought, w*hat's wrong with her? She's ruining her life over a loser, and she could have so many wonderful men who wouldn't beat her and cheat on her. Why does she not understand her value? Do I understand my value?*

Later that day, Sarah walked along the boardwalk with her friend Mira. Mira looked like a model; she had multiple advanced degrees and a successful career running the lab at Huntington Beach Hospital. As they walked, Mira talked about Ben, a guy she'd been hung up on for years. Mira said, "I'm so frustrated; he doesn't make an effort to come see me or make plans for our future." Sarah replied, "You're putting all of your energy into the possibility that someday he will give you the relationship you want, but he has repeatedly showed you that he won't. Why are you investing so much for a guaranteed loss? Would you make that type of investment with your money?" Mira snipped, "No." Then she defended her poor investment with "potential" bullshit.

As Mira talked, the idea that "*love should be the standard*" came to Sarah as she thought *so many times people will not date someone unless they're attractive, educated, same religion, same race, successful, rich, or whatever their standard is. Yet, when describing their "mandatory list," rarely is the word love part of "the standard." They think they can make someone love them.* Sarah was guilty of this as well. She thought, *what if my internal dialogue was he must be capable of loving me or I cannot find him attractive? And I repeated that dialogue over and over. What if "must be capable of love" was more important than all of the other standards?* Other standards are important; of the thousands of conversations she had with individuals sharing what they were looking for, rarely was "love" part of the list. It was assumed, and assumptions are…

At that moment, something clicked, and Sarah realized it is perfectly fine. In most cases, she should reject a person that she doesn't desire, but she had to make sure love shown by consistent actions and behaviors is the number one standard. Sarah had to have the faith to believe that she deserves that kind of love. Holding out for that person did not make her a diva, high maintenance, a dreamer, or unlovable; it meant she realized her value. Did Sarah have an "aha moment" or was she maturing?

With this new perspective, she needed to take a break from dating to understand and solidify her standards. A person can know all the words, "love is patient; love is kind," but love is an action. During her quest to understand what love looks like, she determined the standard should include being able to trust others with the small things so that she could trust them with the big things (like her heart); the standard should also include dependability, reliability, honesty, kindness, loyalty, respect, responsibility, thoughtfulness, generosity, and this person would protect Sarah and her heart. This person would be someone that tries to make her happy. Impulsive people had to go; they could be fun and exciting but were often thoughtless about how their actions impacted others, and they could be emotionally reckless.

Sarah lost her ability to be attracted to a man who wasn't loyal, kind, considerate, and responsible. She didn't have to give up what she was attracted to; she just had to have the patience to have it all, eventually.

16

∞

Broken to Heal

"Every single thing that has ever happened in your life is preparing you for the moment that is to come." –Oprah Winfrey

When Sarah was forty-two she finally figured out "the standard for love", but then she lost all interest in dating. The abuse she endured from the monsters she worked for left her anxious, depressed, and immunocompromised. Sarah also had unexplained weight gain; exercise was unbearable; her skin broke out, and she was in constant pain mainly in her abdomen.

She was home in Huntington Beach, glad to be under the care of Dr. J, her primary doctor. He told her, "I know there's something wrong with you, and we can't find it. I'm so mad at the Specialist who told you there's nothing wrong. When they're not good doctors, they tell you to take a pain pill, eat more fiber, you're just depressed, or you're getting older. This practice is such laziness." She forced herself to work and socialize preferring to be home with her fur babies in her pajamas. She was naturally optimistic and chose to be happy, now she just existed. She seriously questioned God, "Why am I going through such a prolonged period of suffering. Is two years of pain and sickness your way of letting me know I need to make a major change?"

Nursing is an admirable profession, and Sarah worked hard for years giving her best to those she cared for. Over the past couple of years, her cruel bosses took a toll on her, but she was home now working for another great boss like she had so many times, but she was still feeling sick. Her life changed from active to sedentary with her reading more and watching more YouTube videos. Going out was exhausting.

Sarah started deep soul-searching, asking God if she was living the right life. She no longer cared about finding a man; her body ached too much to be touched, let alone have sex. To stay mentally productive, she studied purpose, divine intelligence, manifestations, spiritual development, and how energy impacts individuals. She kept coming across information on failure and vulnerability, topics she never paid attention to before. She had been the first to say "stay positive" not having the insight to realize how insulting this statement was to a suffering person.

She heard J. K. Rowling say, "It is impossible to live without failing at something unless you live so cautiously that you might as well not have lived at all in which case, you fail by default" in a Harvard commencement speech. She thought, *What have I failed at? Romance, I failed in the relationship department, especially with Danny, but that's an easy answer.* The gnawing feeling wondering what she failed at, perhaps by default wouldn't leave her alone. She survived her childhood, put herself through college, traveled much of the world, and had been a devoted nurse since she was twenty-three. She had a lot of friends, done well financially, and wasn't coming up with a great deal of failure. Her Grandma's message "It's time for you to get to work" haunted her. If anything, she was a workaholic, and her Grandma would've told her, "Relax more."

On her three days off, she would go home, put her pajamas on, and stay in them until she had to go back to work. She hired dog walkers and food delivery services to help make her life easier. She continued watching YouTube videos. In one video, she watched Jim Carey say, “You can fail at what you don’t want, so you might as well do what you love.” She read the book *Big Magic* and paid attention to what Elizabeth Gilbert wrote about “ideas” and how we can act on them or they leave us. She had great ideas and set them aside for later; she had been so busy working, traveling, or wasting time in the wrong relationships to give time and energy to her ideas.

In an audio workshop book, Brene Brown, said, “Vulnerability is uncomfortable, uncertainty is like a torture chamber, risk and exposure feel very dangerous. But honestly I don’t know anything more dangerous than standing on the outside of our lives looking in and wondering what it would be like if we showed up, if we really risked and did some of the things that we wanted to do .... I think this is a developmental work of midlife. I think from mid-30s up to maybe 60 even, that this is the developmental challenge. This is when the universe comes down grabs us by the shoulders and says you know I’m not fucking around, this is not, I’m not kidding, this is it, I gave you gifts, I gave you opportunity, I made you in this incredible way and now it’s your turn. And you’re going to have to put the armor down, and you’re going to have to show up and you’re going to have to be brave and you’re going to have to take risk, because it is half way over. ...That’s the challenge for all of us. And I don’t think we can do it without supporting each other and I think that really helps. I think it really helps when you do something really vulnerable or shares something vulnerable and someone looks back and says thanks for sharing that was really brave. It makes a huge difference.” Sarah knew she was coming across all of this information for a reason and suspected it was to connect her to her Grandma's message, "It's time for you to get to work." Even though her body was sick, her spirit was becoming stronger.

She knew she needed to get physically strong because something big was in store; she tried to exercise to produce needed endorphins, but exercise left her exhausted and in excruciating pain. She forced herself to go on a ski trip since skiing was one of her greatest passions; she hoped it would give her the spark she needed. On the lift rides, she dozed off, and at the end of the day, her hip was in unbearable pain; she assumed it was a stress fracture causing the pain.

Although disenchanted with medical care, the pain was so severe that Sarah took an Uber to the emergency department at the hospital she worked at the next morning. She thought as they took her blood and urine, *I'm so embarrassed for my coworkers to see me this vulnerable in this awful hospital gown*. She expected that the Emergency Room Provider would say, "Here's your referral to physical therapy, a prescription for pain medication, don't put weight on your hip." She didn't understand why she wasn't being discharged after the x-rays and the MRI results came back; then they wanted to do a CAT scan. She thought, *they told me there wasn't anything wrong for so long; why are they making a big deal for a fracture?*

Sarah was texting her so-called single "friend" Mira, who worked in the hospital, to give her updates when Diana, her dear friend and a renowned radiologist who supported her through the Justin saga, came into the emergency room. Diana was one of her treasured Angels. With Diana's six kids and busy family outside of work, they only had time for an occasional lunch and volunteer activities, but their sisterly bond remained even as Sarah lived abroad.

Diana kept looking over at her as she was talking to the doctor; then Diana walked over and hugged Sarah as she said, “Hey sweetie, I was surprised to be reading an MRI with your name on it. I had to check on you.” Diana looked concerned and hugged her again. Sarah sensed something was wrong. Diana sat down next to her and held her hand saying, “I think I saw something a little strange on your MRI, and I want to make sure it’s nothing. I asked your doctor to order additional tests; I’m going to take you with me to get an ultrasound now.” Sarah was a bit surprised but not too concerned. She was told, “Nothing is wrong” for so long she believed it.

The ultrasound technician started the procedure as soon as they arrived. Sarah was annoyed at how long the technician was taking as the technician took more and more pictures of her uterus and ovaries, keeping the uncomfortable vaginal probe up her vagina probing in areas with no pain. Diana kept poking her head in as the technician did her best to have a poker face.

Lynn hadn’t responded to Sarah’s calls or texts, so she continued to text Mira updates. Mira was working in the lab two floors below the radiology department and wasn’t that busy. As a friend, she should’ve come up to be with her. They talked on the phone daily, spent holidays together, traveled, shared the single women plights, and had been a big part of each other’s life.

After the technician finished, Diana came in and sat next to her; she’d been crying. Diana took her hand and said, “Honey, you have abnormal growths on your ovaries and uterus that look like they’ve spread, but you have to have more testing. I’ve already arranged for you to be seen by Dr. Deed, a top gynecologist oncologist, tomorrow morning; he owes me a lot of favors. If you don't get this treated right away, it could be bad; you're lucky that your hip started hurting." Sarah was dumbfounded; Diana gave her a big hug and sat with her for a while. "Are you saying I have ovarian cancer?" Sarah asked. Diana looked sad as she wept, "It looks that way maybe uterine cancer as well." Diana was hugely respected, known as "the catcher," because she caught abnormalities after a patient had repeatedly been told she was fine. Diana would look at the images one more time and catch a missed disease. She saved many lives with the extra time and care she put in. Sarah knew Diana was right without additional testing. Ovarian cancer was one of the most deadly. Diana stayed with her until the technicians repeatedly announced, "Several patients are waiting."

Sarah slowly changed into her clothes; her hip was still in pain as she texted Mira to let her know the results of the ultrasound. Mira acted like she cared and texted back, "Let's have lunch and talk about this; it's not good." By the time that Sarah limped down to the cafeteria, Mira was walking out. Sarah was emotionally fragile as she asked Mira, "What about us having lunch?" Mira said, "I already ate; go get your own lunch." Sarah was stunned; she just found out that she had a life-threatening disease; an enemy wouldn't have treated her this bad. Mira then groaned, "I guess I can spend a little bit of time with you" as she turned and walked back in with her.

In shock, Sarah bought her lunch and sat there staring at Mira. She had told Mira what Diana told her a few minutes ago; Mira had several advanced degrees in the medical field; she knew how serious this diagnosis was. Mira pointed at herself saying, "I need to do more stuff for me. I need to focus on me. My life is all about me. I need to take care of me." Sarah was feeling nauseous listening to her. Hearing the word "me" was like hearing a screaming gong. Sarah thought, *how could I have been friends with Mira for so many years when she is so disgustingly selfish?* She sat there in disbelief absolutely speechless as she tried to chew on the dry bread from her sandwich as her rose-colored glasses shattered. All the love she had for Mira, dissipated leaving only feelings of disgust. In that moment, she saw the truth and realized *I've been the only one in this relationship giving anything. How did I miss this? Yeah, we had good conversations, but I must've projected my own goodness onto her and didn't see her for who she is. I thought because we're similar in age, had difficult life circumstances, and are hard-working professional women that we were more alike than we actually are. Now that I'm sick and don't have anything to give in this moment, she is showing her true colors, whatever color disgustingly selfish is.*

Selfishness was so unintuitive to Sarah; she didn't have a strand of selfish DNA and was blind to it. Her friend Julie told her years before "You have so much love to give, and you give and give until somebody knocks you upside the head." She didn't fully agree as she considered herself a good judge of character, but this was a perfect example of what Julie meant.

After lunch, Sarah went to see Dr. J since Diana had taken it upon herself to call him to ask him to see Sarah right away. Diana had connections everywhere. Sarah thought *this is a bit much. I'll see the oncologist tomorrow.* Dr. J immediately greeted her as she was having her vital signs taken, and with his thick Middle Eastern accent, he asked, "How is my favorite healthy girl doing?" Then answered himself, "Not so good." She always liked him; he was a wonderful human being. He saw her many times over the last two years searching for an explanation as to why she ran out of energy and felt so cruddy. He was frustrated and would say, "I've been a doctor for thirty-seven years, and I know there's something wrong. What's wrong with these specialists? I'll send you to a different one." Every appointment they talked about different parts of the world and current events.

Dr. J asked, "Do you know what's going on?" She shook her head, "Yes." They talked for a few minutes, and then he asked her, "Do you mind sitting outside of my office?" As she sat outside his office, she overheard his conversation; he was speaking loudly with intense passion, not his typical demeanor. She heard him say, "We have to get her eggs harvested right away so she can be a mother."

He came out smiling as he said, "Come in, I have good news. You can get your eggs harvested right away so you can still have a baby. Looking at the date of your last cycle, you will be ovulating in a three weeks, I can write you a prescription for fertility drugs to start today and you can harvest your eggs in three weeks. Which appointment do you want?" She hadn't thought about the possibility that she wasn't going to have biological children, so much happened so fast. Dr. J was brilliant and had incredible foresight for her future. He respected her and knew she would be an excellent mother. He repeated, "Which appointment do you want?" She said, "None of them." He shook his head and argued, "I know this is a lot to take in, Sarah, but you want to get your eggs harvested. You want to be a mother. You're going to be such a great mother; the world needs mothers like you. Having children will add so much joy to your life."

She always wanted to be a mother, and if she didn't get pregnant or freeze her eggs within the next few years, she wouldn't be able to have biological children. Dr. J asked again, "You want to get your eggs harvested, right?" Sarah looked at him and said, "No." Her logic was screaming at her, "What are you doing? You've always wanted to be a mother. You could be blowing your chances. You're making the worst decision of your life." Dr. J pleaded with her saying, "I know you, Sarah; you want to be a mother, and you will be such a good mother. You must do this; I know you want children; you are just in shock." In a direct tone, she asserted, "Not like this."

Dr. J told her, "Go home and reconsider." After she left his office, he broke patient confidentiality and called Diana saying, "You need to talk to Sarah; she is in shock and will not get her eggs harvested. She will regret this forever." Diana called her and pleaded with her, "Please get your eggs harvested. You broke up with Justin even though you loved him because you wanted to have kids." Sarah continued to say, "Thank you for your concern; I'm so blessed to have a friend like you, but this is not what I want." Logically, she thought *maybe I lost my mind, but I know I'm making the right decision. I'll be a mother, just not like this,* but that's another story.

She took an Uber home and called her neighbor Beth to make arrangements for Beth's son Ben, her occasional hired dog walker to walk her dogs, Peetee and Tempe. Sarah's hip pain was too painful to walk the dogs. Forty minutes later, she texted Ben, "Where are you? Is everything okay?" Fifteen minutes later, Ben showed up at her house sweating, shaking and crying with just Peetee. Sarah panicked, "What's wrong? Where's Tempe? He cried, "She darted away and got hit by a car." "What, no, no, no! This can't be happening," screamed Sarah. With excruciating hip pain, she ran down the street in disbelief. *How could this be happening? How could something else go wrong? Didn't God know that I have all I can handle?* She wanted to see Tempe. Beth was outside talking to the sheriff as she ran up and sobbed, "Where is she?" The sheriff replied, "It's not a good idea to see her. You'll receive a bill for the animal carcass disposal. Do you want to have her cremated?" He was so insensitive. Beth wrote her address on a piece of paper and handed it to the sheriff saying, "Have her cremated, and then mail her the bill, she'll pay for it." Sarah was thinking, *you selfish, uncaring bitch; you have eaten at my home hundreds of times and never reciprocated. I've done so much for you. I paid your kid to walk my dog and he let her dart into traffic. Perhaps you should take some responsibility?*

She cried until her appointment with Dr. Deed the next day. Dr. Deed informed her, "It looks like you have both endometrial and ovarian cancer and need surgery. I can get you in next month. You'll have chemotherapy so apply for disability; you won't be working." She hadn't thought about the financial impacts this would have.

The next afternoon she received a call from Alan; she rarely talked to him because he had shut himself off and didn't return calls or texts. He sobbed, "Jennifer died." *Oh my God, this is not happening*. Jennifer was one of the few people Sarah stayed in contact with after high school. Jennifer had agoraphobia and wouldn't leave her house, but they talked frequently, and Jennifer was Sarah's cheerleader. Sarah couldn't process what Alan said and asked, "What? I can't believe this? How did she die?" Alan cried, "She had a heart attack, and she was only forty-two. She wasn't overweight." Sarah thought *I'm drowning in waves of emotional pain; how can this be happening?* She cried so much she was afraid she would never stop crying. She learned Jennifer died completely alone. Jennifer had a hard life, lots of abuse, especially sexual, and was estranged from her family. They understood each other. Sarah wasn't sure what made her sadder the loss of a friend, or that her friend died completely alone or that Jennifer had such a sad life? She hated that Jennifer died alone but knew her family hurt her, and she chose to be alone over guaranteed pain. Sarah understood this more than anyone.

This was the darkest period of her life. Her character, spirit, and strength were tested beyond conceivable limits. Throughout the year, four of her friends would die, including Joseph, her favorite mentor who always believed in her. Jennifer's death was the hardest; they were bonded through despondency. Sarah lost more friends to betrayal than death in this season.

Serendipitously, Erica and Matthew were staying with her the night before her first surgery and the first four days afterwards as it coincided with dropping Mercedes off at UCLA to start college. They would be loving and supportive. Lynn was astonishingly aloof as Sarah felt cruddier, less fun, and didn't feel like going out leading up to her diagnosis. Lynn was indifferent when Sarah told her, "I have cancer." Lynn's reaction was devastating to Sarah.

Sarah immediately sensed something was wrong when Erica gave her a cold hug. During the visit, Erica was snobby, shallow, and image obsessed. Being loved was supposed to make you better but not her. Matthew spoiled her and gave her everything; as a result, she became self-centered and materialistic, raising Mercedes the same way. She had no concern about Sarah's diagnosis or the loss of her friends and her dog. Erica made constant demands of Matthew. When Erica was out shopping, Sarah asked Matthew, "What's up?" He just said, "Everything's good." Sarah replied, "I know better; I hate seeing you become a hollow shell of a man."

Sarah waited three hours for Erica to pick her up from the hospital two days after her surgery. When Erica arrived, there was no apology, and she acted annoyed that she agreed to pick Sarah up. Dog urine and feces were on the floor when Sarah returned home, and Peetee seemed traumatized. Erica obviously hadn't cared for him, and Matthew had flown back early. Sarah was so drugged up she thought she perceived the situation differently than it was. She was saving Erica thousands of dollars by letting her stay with her. Putting Peetee out a couple of times a day only took a few minutes.

Sarah was vulnerable and had arranged for help, but Erica insisted other friends come after she left. Erica had benefitted a great deal from her friendship with Sarah; Sarah hosted her repeatedly in both the States and other countries and was always the more generous friend. Erica took Sarah's credit cards to go to the store for needed items throughout her stay. Sarah was in bed healing with extensive surgical incisions; her cancer was possibly terminal, and she slept most of the time. When she would wake up, Peetee had relieved himself on the floor. Sarah wasn't supposed to get out of bed, but she had to take care of him. She wondered if the drugs were making her delusional, and this situation wasn't happening. When Erica left, Sarah's inner voice screamed, "Look in your purse." She opened her wallet finding that two of her credit cards were missing. She called Erica who was loading her car asking, "Have you seen my credit cards?" She wanted to give Erica the benefit of the doubt. Erica came back slamming the cards on the counter saying, "I left them in my pocket after getting your stuff." Then Erica stormed out.

A few hours later, Holly arrived. Sarah met Holly when Holly was working pro bono spearheading a major advertising project for animal welfare. Holly talked Sarah into adopting Tempe. They had a psychic connection straight away. As Holly walked in, she immediately declared, “There’s bad energy here; we must sage ourselves and the house.” Sarah was open to psychic energy and knew Holly had psychic gifts. After Holly saged the entire house, she cooked vegan food for the two of them. Holly rubbed all the knots from Sarah’s back and shoulders from the built-up toxins caused by the surgery and cancer. Sarah and Holly had several deep spiritual chats; Holly’s presence was healing. Sarah told Holly about her experience with Erica, and Holly insisted she check her bank statement. Sarah said, “No, no she would never do that.” Holly insisted, “Just check.” Sarah logged in to her accounts and noticed several charges made during Erica’s visit.

Sarah didn’t know how to process Erica’s betrayal. All Sarah could think was, *How? Why? This doesn’t make sense. I would’ve given Erica the money if she needed it, she did not have to steal from me.* She sat on her couch deeply hurt; she no longer knew Erica. Holly sat next to her and put her hand on her knee as she said, “Not everyone is going to be in your life forever; my intuition is telling me that you’re meant to do something big, and you don’t see it, so there’s no way you can see the people who are holding you back. Not everyone is destined for greatness; if they were, greatness would be average.” She had no idea what “greatness” Holly was talking about.

After Holly left, Katie flew in from Washington, D.C. Katie was a night shift nurse Sarah worked with a short time on a traveling assignment years before, but they stayed in touch. Katie moved to the U.S. when she was twenty-five and taught herself English while taking different jobs to put herself through nursing school. She faced discrimination and was frequently dismissed because of her thick accent. Sarah was grateful for her and felt blessed to recognize how extremely intelligent Katie was. Sarah knew it must have been tremendously difficult to overcome everything Katie had. Katie loved Sarah for seeing her for who she really was. Sarah always went out of her way to overemphasize how intelligent Katie was when she was giving her a reference and reminded others not to overlook her abilities because of her accent. Katie was one of the most generous people Sarah knew, and she dropped everything to spend time with Sarah when she found out Sarah was sick. Katie cooked Sarah the most delicious Vietnamese food along with healing teas and soups. When she left, she said, "Every day you must eat fresh ginger, fresh fruit, and fresh vegetables."

Johnny called daily and visited frequently. He sent packages and made sure Sarah had everything she needed. Lynn never reached out or visited. Sarah didn't know what to do about Lynn but had to focus on her health; she couldn't focus on betrayal or negative energy. She needed all of her strength; her cancer was found in the later stages; chemotherapy was wreaking havoc on her body.

Her first surgery wasn't aggressive enough, and she had two more surgeries before everything was successfully removed; chemotherapy was much worse than surgery. She had never been hospitalized, homebound, or bedridden before this surgery, and as a result, Sarah went into a severe depression. She depended on an active lifestyle to keep the depression demons at bay. As she lay in the hospital bed mostly concerned about Peetee, weeping, running her hands through her hair as it fell out in clumps, with bloody noses, receiving blood transfusions with uncontrollable temperatures of 103-105 Fahrenheit, she prayed to and questioned God. There were times she prayed to die; her quality of life was so bad, and she was so tired of suffering.

She thought about being with her Grandma and how comforting that would be; she missed her horribly and needed her now more than ever. At the peak of Sarah's fevers, she was delusional, and in her delusions, her Grandma would tell her, "You're going to make it, honey. You're going to be stronger than ever; life will be better than you can imagine. Now get to work."

Sarah had an unbelievable hard couple of years; she was shocked and heartbroken over and over. She endured so much pain that she became numb. When Sarah would call Lynn, her best girlfriend of seventeen years, Lynn made comments such as, "I thought before they found the cancer everything was in your head." "Make sure you get out and exercise." "Stay positive." She never came to see her, despite working in the same hospital where Sarah was receiving treatment. Lynn made it repeatedly clear that she was impatient with Sarah's weakness; her lack of support added to Sarah's pain. Sarah had to focus on surviving so she could only process the pain in waves, or it would have consumed her. She didn't understand Lynn's actions towards her. Lynn had made Sarah laugh harder than any other friend; they stood up for each other, pushed each other in nursing school and in all other areas of their lives. They supported each other through heartbreaks, made many stupid mistakes together in their twenties, had so much history and were there for each other. How could Lynn not be there during such a difficult time in Sarah's life?

A year before Sarah was diagnosed, Lynn was ganged raped. The morning after the rape, Sarah intuitively knew something was wrong. Sarah called Lynn from work; she had to hear her voice. Lynn wasn't answering her cell, so Sarah called her at home. Lynn answered the phone in a shaky frail voice, and Sarah asked, "What's going on? I know something is wrong." Lynn started sobbing and was inaudible. Sarah immediately let her boss know she was leaving work for a family emergency. Lynn was her "soul sister." When Sarah arrived at Lynn's house, it was dark and locked up; she used her key to get in. Lynn was in the bedroom closet laying in a fetal position. Sarah sat on the floor and put Lynn's head on her leg to use as a pillow and rubbed her head as she calmly asked, "What happened?" Lynn sobbed, "I don't know. I went to the bar last night and met a guy; we went back to his house, and I kept waking up in different positions with different men on me and in me, sometimes two at the same time." Lynn cried harder sobbing, "I woke up with a beer bottle in my vagina." Sarah gasped and asked, "How did you get out of there?" Lynn replied, "He was sleeping; I put a shirt on and ran home. I just got home when you called." Sarah was worried these men might come after Lynn so that Lynn wouldn't report them. Sarah asked, "Do they know your full name and address?" Lynn replied, "No" as she looked around realizing she left her phone and wallet at the guy's house. Sarah got her out of the house immediately, helped Lynn through all the legal drama that unfolded as Lynn stayed with her until the men were put away in jail. Sarah sat with her while she cried and calmed her after nightmares. It was incomprehensible how Lynn could be so cold and indifferent. Lynn's behavior was devastating to Sarah, but if she was honest with herself, that still small voice, the voice of God that always guided her especially when she was in the hospital bed comforting her, had been letting her know this year would be a year of clearing, pulling weeds, pruning, planting seeds, and having faith. Clearing Lynn out of her inner circle was especially hard. Sarah was okay with pain if she understood the meaning behind it, but she didn't understand this pain.

During her third round of chemo when things were really hard as she lay in the hospital bed shaking with uncontrollable fevers, infections, low blood counts, and the oncology team was sure that she wasn't going to survive. The people Sarah thought would love her and care for her hadn't, and she had a major epiphany and realized she had to love and care for herself completely and unconditionally with an unstoppable passion. This love had to transcend to all areas of her life. She was done worrying about five pounds and was never going to waste time on unsatisfying relationships again. If people or relationships were not enriching her life, she needed to move on grateful for the good times, knowing they were a boost on her way to her destiny, but not part of it. She was only receptive to a good, kind, loving, and giving man she passionately desired.

While fighting for her life, she thought about her Grandma and how much she missed her. She only had her for nineteen years, and Sarah was now forty-two. She never took the time to grieve the loss of her Grandma properly; the pain was so bad she compartmentalized it and focused on her work. Her Grandma was the only one who provided security for Sarah, and when she was gone, Sarah had only herself and her faith. Being forced to slow down made her realize how much she still deeply missed and needed the love from her Grandma. *What would her life be like if her Grandma would have lived? Comforting her over the years and especially now?* Her Grandma symbolizes everything Sarah considered to be home, love, comfort, and stability. She had lavish Christmas parties and celebrated Sarah with unconditional love; she was so loving and generous even when Sarah was a self-centered teenager who didn't appreciate her as she should have. Sarah regretted this. *Was that why she traveled and moved so much taking opportunities not afforded to her Grandma? Or was she running from her own pain?*

Perhaps both? When Sarah moved to a new country, she wished it was her turn to take care of her Grandma showing her the world. She felt her Grandma's spirit over the years; she knew her Grandma was proud of her but couldn't understand why she had visions of her saying "It is time to get to work." If anything, she would've said, "relax and don't be a workaholic."

While lying in bed for weeks at a time, she felt pain on levels she didn't know was possible. She looked at her life choices and actions. While she was proud of most of her life, she had to understand why she was a magnet for selfish people. She asked herself, "How do I not see it until I'm smacked upside the head with their incredible selfishness?" Sarah came to understand that since conception, she was programmed to be used and even though logically she knew it wasn't healthy, what a person knows and how they are programmed can be quite different. She had to break this pattern paying attention to the actions not the words of the people in her life. She had tolerated irrational humiliating outbursts of rage from people who claimed to care for her yet took every opportunity they could to verbally and emotionally beat her down in order to make sure she was an equal. "Equally broken." She accepted she was a threat to many, a mirror of accountability that was too much for some. She stopped allowing people who wouldn't take responsibility for their life into her life.

Romance and sex were the last things on her mind, but it would've been nice to have a loving, supportive companion she could depend on or a family of her own. She and Aden remained close; he called, flew out to see her, and sent flowers after the surgeries.

Sarah had to be broken open time and time again during that period in her life; the pain wasn't going to leave until she learned the lessons she needed to from it. She learned all of her actions and words had to be congruent and in alignment with what she wanted. She took incredible care of herself, spoke lovingly, and had unwavering faith knowing that someday her strength would return. All future relationships must be give-give relationships. She was completely single while she was sick; it was a heartbreaking, sad, and lonely period in her life, but what she needed to be broken open to loving herself like she never had before.

Sarah was now a failure in health and relationships, but she felt like there was something more. She remembered a dream she had when she was working for Cathy, the most destructive demonic dementor; in the dream, she was a tiny white dot on a red flag. She believed that the dream had a powerful meaning. At that time, she pondered for just a second *if nursing was her red flag? How could nursing possibly be a red flag? I'm an excellent nurse with years of advanced training. Nursing is a purposeful profession. What would I do if I wasn't a nurse? I've worked in nursing for nineteen years; have I wasted time? Do I like being a nurse? Is it my passion? What is my passion? Am I burnt out? What is it about nursing that I don't like?* She wondered, *what are my gifts and the opportunities I'm not showing up for? I don't have a lot of joy in nursing, purpose yes, but not passion. I hate all of the paperwork, doing everything in triplicate that takes time away from the patients. Health care is so litigious; we are supposed to treat patients like robots rather than as individuals. I'm not one of those cold, detached nurses like Cathy, the dementor who threatened to write me up when I put my hand on somebody's shoulder as they were crying after their child died. I hate when patients just want to get something or get out of something, not get the care they need. I'm sick of the mentality we have to find what's wrong with this person rather than what's right and the I'm a DOCTOR and you're just a nurse mentality, so your nineteen years of experience do not matter. Every year the suicide rates continued to climb, despite decreased mental health stigma and increased access to care. So what do I love? I love caring for people, making a difference in their lives. I'm an excellent caretaker, teacher, and a natural speaker. When I was healthy, my incredible energy and stamina were empowering to others; I can see so many solutions to problems others don't see; I naturally connect with people. I love traveling, being active, rescuing and rehabilitating animals, and I know the importance of giving and doing for others. Perhaps these are the gifts Brene Brown was talking about.*

Prolonged suffering made Sarah willing to have her mind and heart open to the opportunities that were in alignment with the incredible way she was made. She wasn't sure what she was going to do, but a dream and a vision were starting to come together. Most people couldn't understand this vision she was starting to see. Finally! She figured it out; she was failing herself, playing it so cautiously that she continued staying in a job she had long ago outgrown and become burnt out in because it was a secure job. She tried to lie to herself saying, "Having a purpose in a job was enough." But that no longer worked. She would have to step in the arena of her life; it was time for her to be her own narrator and figure out what she was passionate about, even if she failed terribly.

After the cancer was undetectable, she and Peetee moved to Puerto Rico and bounced all over the Caribbean Islands for a year living with just the essentials using her rental income, investments, and even though she strongly objected money from Johnny to support herself. She was Johnny's best and most loyal friend for almost twenty years; he wanted her healthy and happy, so she would be in his life for another forty years.

She slept a lot, practiced yoga, swam in the warm water, started running again, ate healthy organic fresh fruit and vegetables, and relaxed. Her imagination ran wild and she was present while she talked to people with no agenda or purpose; she started to have fun again.

After living in the Caribbean Islands, she traveled the world in between running the Albatros Adventure Marathons. As she ran, her dreams and destiny became clearer. After a year devoted to becoming as healthy as possible, followed by a year of pushing herself to the limits physically, she, much like the Phoenix rises from the ashes, rose stronger, more energetic and wiser than before. She was ready to fulfill her destiny and knew it would unfold as she stepped into the unknown.

17

∞

Timing and Faith

"I learned to trust my instincts." –Ralph Lauren

Taking time to recharge, Sarah let her imagination run wild, strengthening her to honor her gifts. The abuse she endured from the bullies she worked for left her more compassionate towards the vulnerable and voiceless, especially foster children and animals.

When she returned to the States, she worked part-time and took short travel assignments to support herself. Her infectious energy returned, and she accepted offers to work as a consultant. As part of her job, she went to hospitals and organizations to address what wasn't working when it came to suicide prevention and relationships. She talked to mental health professionals, educators as well as other health care providers about how they unknowingly enable rather than empower people to become the best version of themselves. Her energy, life experiences, travels, and near-death experiences were captivating; she was in demand.

Sarah did public speaking on empowerment while being sensitive to individuals who were powerless because they were being abused or bullied and were not in a place to be helped. She started anti-bullying campaigns, exposed bullies, and went to schools in the most impoverished areas, meeting great kids with so much potential who needed something (different for everyone) to start a flicker of hope.

Her years of working in mental health taught her to adjust her approach for each individual she encountered, but this wasn't an option when speaking to large groups. In the ghettos, the students were shocked at how they misjudged her with their first impressions. She easily commanded a room regardless of the audience, talking about hope and how we become what we believe. She searched the crowd for the students that looked like they would have low self-esteem and asked them to be her volunteer assistant. If they agreed the volunteer would sit on stage, and Sarah would say, "Tell me about your dreams." The student often described a dream so small it was barely above existing. She would then describe an amazing life about a person who had everything he always wanted and say, "What kind of person has that life?" Usually, the student volunteer described someone from a good family, neighborhood with the best schools, someone everybody loved with an easy life.

She, of course, had set them up and then the more aggressive not so nice side of her came out as she challenged their mind set and talked about entitlement, struggle, and pain. She hated entitled mindsets in those who never worked or struggled for anything, yet they felt they were entitled to everything. She shocked the kids when she would get in their faces and say, "Tell me about an amazing person who you admire that had a perfectly charmed life and never had anything bad happen to her?" Of course, they couldn't. She went on to say, "So that rich kid from the perfect family living in the perfect home who never had to struggle, is that who you admire? You want a life with no struggle? Why does an entitled bitch who has never worked a day in her life, whose major life crisis is not getting the spa appointment she wants, get everything she wants? Is it because she BELIEVES she is entitled to it? I know life can be hard. It is not okay that you're being abused, and believe me, I know that there are some of you in this audience who are being abused right now and that is NOT OKAY; I pray you're able to get help. You might be in a place right now where you feel powerless, but that will not last. You get in life what you believe. If you're entitled and never struggle, but you get the car and house you want, it is because that is what you believed you deserved. If you live in the ghetto and have low expectations for life, that is going to be what you get because that is what you believe. However, for those of you who are suffering and struggling, you actually have a better chance for greatness than those who have life handed to them. There's not a single interesting person who has not had to struggle; the adversity and suffering that you overcome is what makes you interesting." She also reminded the students that "We all have struggles, but some don't have near as much to overcome."

Her approach of appearing like a gentle, soft-spoken woman and then turning into an aggressive in your face tough cookie that wouldn't back down was extremely effective with her audiences. She had a way of challenging the bullshit they listened to and told themselves. Her speeches could be loud and aggressive; but she was soft-spoken and gentle when she was talking one on one. The stories she heard about abuse filled her with rage, and she incorporated bully exposure into her speeches. Examples of abusers being held accountable validated the victims. Her speeches garnered attention and the demand for her speaking engagements grew. She had large speeches to give in Baltimore, MD, Philadelphia, PA, and Washington D.C. before taking a break to recharge.

Johnny was inspired to take a break from his workaholic life and came to support his best friend as she stepped into this unknown uncharted chapter of life as well as to celebrate their birthdays. For their birthdays, they went to the Top of the Tower in Philadelphia for some fine dining, panoramic views, and spectacular ambience. Johnny looked at her and said, "Sarah, I've been worried about you. I'm afraid you've completely given up on love." He was intuitive and looked out for her best interests. He went on to say, "I love and support you no matter what. You're the strongest person I know, but even strong people need a helper. I wonder if you're ever going to share your life with someone? I want the best for you."

She smiled saying, "I'm happier now than I have been in years. I've so much passion in my life; I'm alive and elated with how my life's evolving. I don't want distractions." He then insisted, "You have lived an exceptional life; you weren't supposed to live, and you did. Don't you believe that you will have an exceptional relationship? I know you will be part of the 10 percent of the happy couples." There was silence then he asked, "Well, wouldn't you want that?" Sarah laughed, "Yeah right! I'm forty-seven. Life has taught me I'm good single. I like being single." Then she paused and then said, "I've had weird signs though and wondered if that was God's way of saying, "The person you're meant to be with is on the way."

Johnny questioned, "Tell me about the signs?" She didn't care how silly she sounded; she beat cancer; besides he was her most trusted confidant who loved her unconditionally. She told him, "I prayed for God to take the desire for a man out of my heart until the right one comes along, since then I've not met anyone I'm the least bit interested in. But I see the name Gabriel everywhere; sometimes I meet three different men named Gabriel in a day. Do you remember the Gabriel story? I've always had a strong feeling I was meant to be with him, and I don't even know him. Diana is still certain Justin and I will get back together, but I have no interest. Then I think maybe I'll see Caleb again and see men with curly brown hair everywhere; I suspect Caleb and Gabriel have similar occupations and maybe that's the Gabriel connection. Then Aden will call; he is such a great man, and I admire and respect him so much. He gives me hope that there are amazing single men out there, but nothing has happened between us. Maybe I'm crazy." Then she laughed, "If I could meet a man who loved me as much as you love your work that would be a miracle….I'm joking. I'm forever appreciative of you and for all you have done for me. I love you and I am beyond blessed to have you as my best friend."

He could tell she was trying to change the subject, so he persisted, "Be serious, Sarah. I know you have a list. What do you want in a man?" She replied, "Okay, here's my list of non-negotiables; if somebody was to be my very sexy puppy, he must meet everything on my list:

"Must love and desire me for who I am in all my forms. Respect for God. It is only by the grace of God that I'm alive, and he has to appreciate that. Give me space and alone time, and he must be okay being alone at times too. He must have an honorable character and be respectful even when we don't agree. I have to be physically attracted to him; I'm attracted to well-built, muscular men similar in age who are motivated to be healthy, no tobacco! Hard balanced worker, be his own man and understand I really am my own woman. He cannot be overly jealous and must be secure with himself, independent but also wants to share his life with me. Intelligent and financially secure. He has to be kind and appreciate my kindness and not take me for granted. Good personality, open-minded, with world experience so we can relate. Faithful and loyal and I want him to pursue me."

Johnny stared at her insisting, "Well, you're going to have to settle on some of those; it's just not realistic" Sarah snapped, "What should I settle on? A good personality? Fidelity? Should I date someone that does not take care of himself? Should I be with somebody I'm ashamed of? Should I be with someone who is not supportive? How about if I date a broke loser? Or somebody who is mean and jealous? Somebody lazy? Someone I can't stand to look at or to touch me? What should I settle on? What one of those would you settle on?"

Johnny was caught off guard but realized her tone wasn't directed at him but the years of pressure to settle. He thought about it and responded, "None, I guess." Then he went on to say, "Well, I'm going to see if I can find a guy for you." Sarah replied, "No thanks! I'm good."

After dinner, she gave him a big hug goodbye and told him how grateful she was for him again. Then texted Derrick confirming, "I'm on my way, I'll be at your house tonight." The next day Derrick asked, "You want to go to the gym for old times?" She laughed, "Sure." At the gym, she had flashbacks of Gabriel finishing a set of pull-ups with weights strapped around his waist and scanned the gym, but he wasn't there.

After her speech in D. C., she and her current rescue babies Hope and Faith were ready for some downtime. She wasn't sure what she'd do as she recharged over the next month but glad she was free to do what she wanted. She hugged and thanked Derrick and his husband, Brent, for letting her, Hope and Faith stay as Derrick and Brent dropped them off at the metro. While waiting for the metro, Sarah said a prayer, "God, thank you that my season of joy has come, that my life is blessed, and I'm stronger and healthier at forty-seven than I've been in years. Give me the wisdom on how to use my blessings and the strength and courage to help others. I know I'm at the beginning steps of turning the suffering and abuse I endured from the bullies into something great as I speak out and expose bullies to minimize the suffering for others. Help the scared bullies that underestimated me as I begin my journey to decimate them." As she continued to look to the heavens praying for wisdom on how to handle the *Scared Bullies with Power and Control,* there was a tap on her shoulder.

She turned around to see Gabriel smiling at her. Her heart stopped, and when it restarted, it raced at two hundred beats per minute. Fortunately, she was finally able to discipline her emotions enough to remain calm as the interest she had prayed for came back like a dam that burst from excessive pressure. She smiled back, and he said, "I remember you; I've searched for you. You're truly a woman on the move." They laughed; then he asked, "What's going on with you?" She beamed saying, "Well, I'm getting ready to take on some *Scared Bullies with Power and Control."*

∞

Now It Is Your Turn

Dearest Reader!

I hoped you enjoyed reading *Single, Pitiful, and Unlovable…Yeah Right!* and feel inspired knowing you're right where you are supposed to be. If you need to step up to be the best version of yourself, get busy and don't settle.

Don't forget to share this book with anybody who could use the encouragement, and please support authors by leaving your needed reviews on:

Amazon

Barnes and Noble

Good Reads

iBookstore

Thank you and Best Wishes,

Jamie

P.S. This is book 2/4 in the Sarah Saga. Sarah and her friends' journey will continue in *Scared Bullies with Power and Control.*

Sarah Saga

Book 1- Why You Tried to Kill Yourself

Book 2- Single, Pitiful and Unlovable…Yeah Right!

Book 3- Scared Bullies with Power and Control

Book 4- ☺ You will have to wait and see what that title will be.

Made in the USA
San Bernardino, CA
17 December 2018